MIKA

EMBER TOWN SERIES
BOOK 4

MJ JAMES

Editor services provided by Rebecca Scharpf at Scrollwork Edits

Proofreading editor services provided by Skey Alley

Cover design by MJ James

ebook ISBN: 978-1-958175-21-7

paperback ISBN: 978-1-958175-40-8

PRAISE FOR MJ JAMES

James's effective worldbuilding employs strong emotional and sensory descriptions ... often paralleling our society's own issues with neurodivergence, gender equality, economic disparity, and more.

THE BOOKLIFE PRIZE ON THE IMMORTAL PART OF MYSELF

Good world-building and a storyline I was quickly hooked into.

GOODREADS REVIEWER ON IN-BETWEEN

To everyone trying to survive

TRIGGER WARNING

The concept of Mika started from seeing an idea about a binary magic ritual. Except gender isn't binary. What would happen if a witch was a lesbian? Then that witch fell in love with a non-binary nymph. Since then, things have changed even more in the world outside my novel. It is more important than ever to see queer representation.

Mika Contains

Adoption: An adult adopted as a child

Misgendering

Homophobia

ALSO BY MJ JAMES

In-Between

The Immortal Part of Myself

NeurodiVeRse

The Ember Town Series

Lucas

Phoenix

Birk

Mika

Lennon

"I can continue to lead the coven," Robert said.

Mika watched his arms move as he spoke. His cheeks and the bald center of his head were both flushed from his passion, or the heat of the council chamber. The elders liked the room to stay warm. His blue robes swished around his slender frame as he gestured, showing off the protruding abdomen he had developed with age.

"Now more than ever we need a strong leader, and Mika isn't ready yet. The Mabon ritual showed that," he continued.

Robert turned to Mika, his eyes seeming to soften, though Mika knew better. It was a good move on his part bringing up Mabon. Mika had tried to call up the magick and bless the harvest, but had taken one look at Rob—Robert's son and her eventual groom—and thought about Birk. The magick had slipped away and Robert and his wife had stepped in to complete the ritual.

"We all know Mika has power," Robert said. "That is why the coven brought her here, but until she accepts the gift given to her, it is best that I stay on as coven leader."

Robert finished with a flourish. He paused as if waiting for a round of applause. Instead, he was met with a loud snore from Elder Milton.

"Don't be silly," Elder Nam said. "You have been in your role for too long already. You have earned your right to join the elders."

The elders sat on a platform built into the corner of the large, and nearly empty, coven chamber. There were currently four elders sitting in their individual chairs. Each chair had a high back and plush cushioning to support their aged frames. It made them look like royalty gazing down at their petitioners. The reality wasn't too far off. The coven leader might lead the rituals and sit on the council, but every major decision had to be approved by the elders.

"I'm hardly old enough to join the council," Robert said. "It's nearly two decades before my eightieth birthday."

"Don't be dense," Elder Nam said. "You know coven leaders join the elders as soon as they step down. We can use some youth up here."

Elder Nam was the oldest member of the elders. At a hundred and nine, she had been an elder almost as long as Mika had been alive. Witches don't live longer than their non-magickal human counterparts, but Elder Nam seemed hell-bent on trying to change that. Her body had grown frail with age, her head bending under the weight of her white-braided hair, but her mind was as sharp and strong as ever.

"Youth!" Elder Emily shouted. She sat next to Elder Nam, her plump frame a stark contrast. At eighty-nine she was currently the youngest elder, but over the last few years, she had started mentally declining and now just repeated what others said.

Mika started inching backward toward the door that led outside. She moved slowly, hoping none of the elders noticed before she was gone. The meeting had already droned on longer than expected and she had a date to get ready for. In just three hours, Mika would finally be going on her first official date with Birk.

"Where do you think you're going?" Elder Sage asked.

"She is trying to sneak off just like she did at Mabon," Elder Nan said. "It was disrespectful. She left right after the ceremony. Coven leaders need to be involved. They should be out talking to the people, determining their needs. I remember when coven leaders were the first to arrive at a ceremony and the last to leave. Her behavior was a disgrace."

"Disgrace," Elder Emily said.

Mika stopped moving after having managed to make it only a few feet away from the door before getting caught. She crossed her arms and tried not to scowl. After all, she was in her mid-thirties, a grown woman destined to be the next coven leader, and she was being talked to like a child.

"I am sure she had a good reason," Elder Sage said. The third elder had been the coven leader before Robert, and at ninety-three, she still went for a brisk walk every morning. "Rob left early also. I'm sure we can imagine what they were getting up to."

Elder Sage reached over and nudged her husband, Elder Milton. He woke up, looked around, and then started nodding his agreement before falling back asleep.

Mika hadn't known that Rob had also left early, although it wasn't surprising. He hated the attention he got from being the betrothed of the coven leader. He was destined to be her husband, to live his life as an addition to her without his own identity. Mika looked at Elder Milton, who had lived the same fate, and wondered if he would go back and change things if given the chance. Neither Mika nor Rob wanted to get married, but that didn't seem to matter to anyone but them.

Wherever Rob had gone, it wasn't with Mika because she had slipped away to attend Birk's housewarming party. Mika couldn't help the flush that came over her at remembering the dance they had shared—and the kiss. It had been a perfect moment. They could create another one in just three more hours when she saw Birk again—if she ever escaped the elders.

"Rob was home alone," Robert said. "When I came home, after staying and cleaning up the ritual, I found him asleep in his room."

"I'm sure he needed his rest," Elder Sage said as she slapped her husband on the back, startling him awake again. "Oh, to be young and in love. I remember what Milton and I used to get up to when we were their age."

"I can assure you that the two weren't together." Robert glanced back at Mika as he spoke, a glint in his eye.

He knew. Somehow, the man had to know about Birk. Mika thought back over the last month. She had been so careful to stay distant from Birk anytime another witch was around. Yes, she'd spoken passionately at the council meeting when Birk was sick, but Mika was a passionate person. Who wouldn't be angry if someone was being poisoned?

Mika looked at the smug expression on Robert's face. The elders leaned forward, as much as their bodies would allow, seemingly eager for any gossip they could get. Mika let out a sigh and decided honesty was the best way to go … well, mostly.

"I left the ritual early because a friend was having a housewarming party. I know everyone is concerned about my limited friendships and decided it was for the good of the coven that I attend." No one had ever mentioned Mika's lack of friendships before, but it seemed like something that would possibly sway the elders.

"A housewarming party on Mabon?" Elder Nam asked.

"I've never heard of such a thing. Housewarming parties should happen in spring. Maybe late fall in a pinch, but Mabon?" Elder Sage said.

"Mabon," Elder Emily said, then stood up and walked to the side of the platform that led to the elders' quarters. The people in the room paused as Elder Emily opened the door and stepped out of view.

She was only gone for a few moments before she reappeared, followed by the elders' caretaker. Tom was a few years younger than Mika. They hadn't interacted much until he'd taken over as primary caregiver. He was a large man, towering over six and a half feet, with a solid build that made it easy to assist the elders as needed. His face, what could be seen under his long, wiry beard, was rounded. His eyes were a bright blue that were crinkled in concern.

Tom was quiet as he stayed behind Elder Emily, his demeanor gentle as he escorted her back to her chair. His arms supported her frame as she climbed back up on the chair and sat down. Before Tom could leave, Elder Emily reached out and gave him a giant hug. His hands wrapped gently around the elder until she let go.

Tom looked at all the elders, seemingly satisfied that they were well, before walking back to the chamber door. He gave a warning glance at Robert and Mika, as if reminding them to take care of the elders in his absence, before disappearing through the doorframe, closing the door softly behind him.

"What self-respecting witch has a housewarming party on Mabon, the night of a harvest ritual?" Elder Nam continued, as if there hadn't been any disruption. "That is a night to give thanks for the bounty the earth has given us. There shouldn't be any side parties happening. We are all one coven and should act accordingly."

"Well," Mika started but stopped, uncertain how to continue.

"Well," Elder Emily said.

Robert looked at her with a smirk of satisfaction and Mika knew that one way or another the information would come out. It was probably best that it came directly from her.

"The housewarming party wasn't hosted by a witch," Mika reluctantly admitted. "It was hosted by a nymph."

"A nymph?" Elder Sage questioned. "Why would a nymph have a housewarming celebration? Don't they live in the woods with their trees?"

Eldar Nam was speechless, something Mika had rarely seen. But the rage seemed to be building, her eyebrows pinching together and her lips scrunching up. Mika glanced back at the exit, wondering if she should make a run for it; the elders wouldn't be able to catch her. However, they would just send for her again. There was no escaping them when they wanted your attention. Mika turned back around and waited for the onslaught. It didn't take long.

"You left your coven to attend to a non-witch on a ritual night?" Elder Nam's voice was steady, but it had a hardness to it that was not normally there.

"I was embarrassed," Mika said. It wasn't *completely* a lie. She had been embarrassed that she had failed the ritual, but that was not the reason she had gone to meet up with Birk. The nymph had a way of twisting up her insides since the first moment she had laid eyes on them in Rocko's bar. It was in their wonder for the world and the compassion they expressed even in their lowest moments. The fact that they were the most gorgeous being Mika had ever seen didn't help either. It was hard to ignore a part of yourself when it refused to be hidden. There had to be a way for the elders to understand. She looked at Elder Sage and Elder Milton and thought maybe if she appealed to their love, their connection, they could see that the way she cared for Birk was no different. But before she could get the words out, Elder Nam spoke again.

"You *should* be embarrassed. You were supposed to have taken over as coven leader years ago. I was there when they found you in that foster home, less than a year old, having just lost your parents. We felt your potential then, and we adopted you and brought you home to your family. It is your destiny to lead the coven. Do you doubt that?"

Mike and Sandra had adopted her. They were witches who had raised her for the coven, but Mika always knew that there was a price to be paid for that kindness. A price the elders pointed out at every opportunity. Mika was grateful, but sometimes she started to wonder who she would have become if they had just left her alone. Those thoughts were unappreciative. She'd had an amazing childhood with lots of love and everything she could ever need. Now, it was her turn to pay it back.

"No, ma'am," Mika said.

"Then please tell us why it was so important that you leave your family to attend to this nymph."

"Well," Mika said. "It is just that Birk had lost their family, and they needed people to support them."

Mika knew as soon as the words left her mouth that they were the wrong thing to say. Robert's face lit up, and his lips curled into a maleficent grin.

"Who is Birk?" Elder Nam asked.

"Isn't that Elowen's daughter, the one who got kicked out?" Elder Sage said.

Mika could picture Birk's reaction to being misgendered.

They tried not to let it show, but every time it happened, they sunk into themselves. Their shoulders hunched, and their face flashed with pain before they attempted to cover it up. Birk may not have been here now, but Mika knew it was her obligation to help the elders to understand.

"Birk is Elowen's child," she said.

"That is what Elder Sage said. You don't need to repeat it. Why was she kicked out of her family?"

"Birk is agender," Mika said. "Their pronouns are they/them. They are not a daughter. They are a child. They are not a she. They are a they."

"What nonsense is this?" Elder Nam said.

"It's these kids. They have lost their way," Elder Sage said. "They don't understand everything that we fought for. I was only the second female coven leader. The first was a few generations before me, and that was only because they didn't have anyone else strong enough to fill the role. She didn't even have authority. Her husband decided everything for her. They made the same suggestion for me. Can you imagine it, Milton, you having a say over what I did? Thankfully, we knew better then. We know how important it is to have the female aspects to help balance out the male ones. That is why I implemented the new policy to alternate genders of coven leaders. We need to maintain our balance. I hope you understand how important your role is."

"I do," Mika said.

"Please tell me you do not subscribe to this dissolution of gender."

"I'm female, if that is what you mean. But it isn't a dissolution of gender; it is just an understanding that gender is more than one or the other. Gender is a spectrum. People's gender fall in different places, and it isn't always in a consistent place."

"Magick is the reaction of opposites." Elder Sage's voice sounded like an upset parent who was trying to teach their child to do better. "It is the combination of these opposites that come together in magickal humans to create the reactions that help our community to thrive. That is why it requires a partnership to perform the rituals—male and female—one more magickal and the other less so. If what you say was true, then magick would not function. There is only male, female, and the partnership between the two."

"Why?" Mika asked.

"Why? Why is the world round or the sky blue? Mother Earth does what she will, and we follow her command."

"Hasn't there ever been a coven leader who didn't marry?" It was as close as Mika could get to asking what she wanted to know. Had there ever been a coven leader who was gay, who loved other women or other men? Or was she the only one? Had she been brought as a child into a family of people who were all straight?

"Not married?" Elder Nam said. "What nonsense are you talking about? Rob and you are fond enough of each other; love will grow in time. If not love, then respect and companionship. You do not need to worry, child."

"I hate to bring this to the elders' attention," Robert said. His face was still beaming, and Mika clasped her hands, worried about what was coming next. "I typically stay out of private matters, but as this involves my son and our next coven leader, I think it is important to let you all know that there have been rumors going around about a potential relationship between Mika and Birk."

"Relationship." Elder Emily squealed.

Elder Sage moved her hand to her mouth with a dramatic exclamation, while Elder Nam became so peaked Mika became concerned. She was about to call for Tom when the older woman spoke.

"I know there have been concerns in the past. They were tolerated to some degree when you were younger. Experimenting with other women isn't completely unheard of, but one grows out of it. You are well past adulthood, and this should not be continuing."

"It wasn't with any woman," Elder Sage said. "It was with a woman who denies being female, enough so that she lost her entire family because of it. She chose her delusion over her family. Are you two involved?"

Mika wasn't sure what to say. She wanted to be involved with Birk, but they hadn't done more than share a kiss. They hadn't even gone on a date yet, and given the length and tone of this meeting, Mika wasn't sure that would ever happen. The room began to feel small, the walls closing in on her. She wanted to get away, but the door suddenly seemed impossibly far.

"We are friends," she finally managed.

"Friends?" Elder Nam said.

"Do you still have feelings for other women?" Elder Sage asked.

"I …" The words died on her tongue. She couldn't bring herself to say no and lie to the elders and denounce a part of herself that she was finally starting to understand. However, she also couldn't tell them and lose the only family that she had known. So, she stood there rubbing her hands up and down her arms even though she wasn't cold.

"It is time for you to put away childish things," Elder Nam said. "We have pampered you for far too long. You need to grow up and accept the mantle of coven leader, and to do that you need to earn the respect of magick by showing it you understand the rules of nature."

"It seems to me that magick respects people for who they are just fine. It is people who go about expecting others to change who they are." Elder Milton's voice was deep but quiet. Mika hadn't even realized that he had woken up, and she couldn't remember the last time he had spoken. His words wrapped around her like their own kind of spell, and she stood up straighter and let her arms fall to her sides.

"Oh, that's a bunch of hodgepodge," Elder Sage said. "Don't worry about what is happening. Go back to sleep and let the women handle this. We have a plan. Elder Nam, don't you think it is time for the plan?"

"Hodgepodge," Elder Emily said.

"I understand your concern," Robert said. He moved in front of Mika, closer to the stage. "It is past time for Mika to work out these feelings that she continues to express, but we have seen that until she does that, she will be unable to control the magick. I want to assure the elders that I have many more solid years left in me as coven leader before I will need to step down. I am sure the Mabon ritual put any concerns you may have had about my continued fitness to rest."

"Yes, you are doing a fine job," Elder Nam said. "But you have held the position a decade longer than you should have. We appreciate your service to the coven, but it is past time for the next coven leader to take over."

"Everything requires balance," Elder Sage said. "And we are tipping the balance over too far one way. If we do not switch leaders soon, then we will go back to the days when only males led."

"We have a plan." Elder Nam leaned forward as she spoke.

"We had hoped that it would not come to this," Elder Sage said.

"It seems that we have no choice," Elder Nam said. "The next ritual is Samhain. Mika and Rob will marry that morning, and then after, she will lead the ritual, finally taking her place as coven leader."

"It will bring balance," Elder Sage said.

"Balance," Elder Emily said.

The room started to spin, and Mika tried to reach out for something, anything to hold on to, but there was nothing around to ground her. "What if I can't?"

"You will," Elder Sage said. "The magick will come because it will know that you are finally bound to be together. That is what is missing."

But Mika wasn't concerned about the ritual; it was the wedding she wasn't sure she could move forward with. She made eye contact with Elder Milton. He looked at her with pity and helplessness. Mika knew that there was nothing he could do. He had spent too much of his life living for his wife's needs to be able to separate himself from them now. So, Mika stared at the ground and tried not to cry.

"This is unnecessarily harsh," Robert said.

Mika looked up at him. He was the last person she had expected to come to her defense.

"No one should be forced into a union. All they need is a little more time. I can give that to them. There is no reason this needs to happen so soon. Samhain is just weeks away."

"Sometimes people need a little assistance to get to where they need to be. It worked out well for you. Besides, I am old. I will not be here much longer, and this needs to get sorted out before I go."

"You will live forever, Elder Nam," Robert said. "Even death knows to leave you alone."

"I have had enough foolishness for one night. Mika will marry and take over as coven leader. I cannot leave knowing that there are only three here to guide the next generation, especially with Elder Emily unable to contribute her wisdom. If all is blessed, we will have our next elder here in another five years. I will not live to see it. You must be up here helping to make sure the coven continues."

"Yes, elder," Robert said. All the fight had gone out of his body.

Elder Nam reached into the side of her blouse and pulled a bell out of a hidden pocket. She rang it twice before the side door opened, and Tom walked out. Mika and Robert waited as each elder was escorted back to their quarters one at a time. When the side door closed behind the last elder, Robert turned to Mika.

"I guess you better go and break up with your *friend*. I will let your fiancé know all about the arrangement." Then he stormed off to the exit, leaving Mika frozen to her spot.

Mika knocked on Birk's door. Her mind was a jumble of everything that had happened, but her thoughts kept focusing on having to tell Birk about her upcoming marriage. Then the door opened, and Mika's mind went blank. Birk was dressed in purple suit pants with a matching purple vest. They wore a white button-down shirt and had on a slightly darker purple tie. Their hair was freshly cut, with one side freshly shaved and the other half perfectly styled in polished, messy perfection. Birk had even applied a small amount of blush and lip gloss that left their lips shiny, and so tempting.

"I'm sorry I'm late," Mika said. She looked down at her outfit, a simple multicolored cotton crinkled skirt, and a simple black blouse. She hadn't gone home after the meeting with the elders. Instead, she'd sat in her car for over an hour, her phone in her hands. Mika had started to text Birk a hundred times and had finally decided that she would tell them in person. "There was a coven meeting that ran late. I didn't have time to go home and change."

"You look amazing," Birk said.

Mika stood there awkwardly. She wanted to walk over to Birk and hold them in her arms and kiss them once again, but she couldn't, not now. Instead, she looked over the living room, which had only changed slightly since Mika had last been there. "How are you settling in?"

"I'm not used to all the quiet. When I lived with my family, all I could think about was getting away and finding my own space. Now I have an entire house to myself, and I can't wait to see other people again."

Mika put her hand in her pocket and felt her car keys. She couldn't imagine being so far out here, away from the town, unable to walk wherever she needed. Guilt at the thought of leaving Birk all alone tonight flared through her. "Have you thought about getting your driver's license?"

"Actually," Birk said as they moved closer to Mika, their hand touching her arm, "the council gave me one, but I still have to practice. Dave is going to pick me up later in the week to teach me. His husband offered, but I couldn't imagine driving that monster of a truck."

Mika felt Birk's hand on her arm. It was warm and solid, and she never wanted them to let go. She moved her hand up to capture Birk's, interlocking their fingers together.

"How does dinner sound?" she asked.

"If you are tired, we can stay in. I got a TV last week. I can cook, and we can put on a movie."

"That sounds fantastic, but I'm guessing you haven't had a chance to leave this house in a while. Let's go somewhere where you can be around other people for a bit."

"That would be wonderful."

Mika led Birk to her car, a small red hatchback that she barely had reason to use. She opened the passenger door for Birk and watched as they slid into the seat. When they winked at Mika, a small smile made it to her lips, and for a moment, every other worry slipped away.

"Where are we going?" Birk asked.

"It's a secret. I wanted our first date to be special."

"Of course it's special—I am with you." Birk rested their

hand on the seat divider, and Mika reached out, clasping their hands together again. She wished she'd never have to let go.

The restaurant was in the southeast part of town, where all the humans tended to settle. It was one of the few human-run businesses in Ember. The owner wasn't even vampire kin, just one of the few that had moved in, unaware that they lived among the magickal. Mika had picked it because she knew they wouldn't have to hide here. Also, Mika thought that Birk's obsession with pizza might make them favor Italian. She had been planning this night since Mabon, wanting everything to be perfect. It was supposed to be a new start, but instead, it was turning into an ending of something that had never been allowed to be.

"Should we go in?" Birk asked.

Mika realized that they had been sitting in the parking lot with the car running for several minutes. She was trying to put off the inevitable. Once they were inside, Mika would have to tell them the truth. She turned and saw the concern on Birk's face and decided that it could wait at least a few minutes. It wouldn't be fair to ruin Birk's dinner.

"Yes, let's go in." She tried to put a smile on her face but wasn't sure she succeeded.

At the front of the restaurant, they were greeted and escorted to a table. It seemed to be a quiet night. However, it was hard to be sure with the low lighting, the background music, and the walls sectioning off tables. They were put at a table for two in a section of the restaurant all by themselves. The tables were covered in white tablecloths with nice imitation crystal glasses.

Birk pulled out Mika's chair for her and then walked over to their own. The host poured them both some water and handed them menus before letting them know that their waiter would be with them shortly.

"Everything looks so good," Birk said, looking over the menu. "It's all so different."

"I wasn't sure if Rocko had introduced you to Italian or not, but since you love pizza so much, I thought you might enjoy this as well."

"This is perfect. I haven't been anywhere this fancy before."

Mika forgot about the menu in her hands and watched as Birk read through all the options. They looked intently at the food choices. Occasionally, their lips pinched together when they found an item. Other times, their eyes lit up. When they had finished reading through the entire menu, they looked up at Mika and found her watching them.

"Did you decide what you want to eat?"

"There is so much to choose from. I don't know what to pick. What are you having?"

Mika looked down briefly at her menu, picking out the first thing she saw.

"I think I'll have spaghetti and meatballs. You can't go wrong with a classic. You know that you can order more than one thing. If you don't eat it all, they will put it in containers for you to take home, and you can have leftovers for the rest of the week."

"That's okay," Birk said. "I'll just order a different item the next time we come here."

Mika felt the joy rush out of her and the reality of the situation took its place. This would be the last time, the only time, that she would be here with Birk. She knew it wasn't fair for her not to speak up, but she also couldn't bring herself to say the words. Once she did, they would somehow be real.

"What's wrong?" Birk asked.

"It's nothing. I wonder what is taking the waiter so long to come take our order. It isn't like there are a whole lot of people needing their attention."

"That's not very nice," Birk said. "I'm sure they will be here as soon as they can."

"Yeah." Mika pulled up the menu and pretended to look at the choices.

"Did you hear back from any of the covens?"

"What?" Mika met Birk's eyes, trying to focus on what they had just asked.

"The letters that you sent out to the other covens asking them about how they practice magick. Did you get a response?"

"No," Mika said. "Magick is binary. It requires two opposite forces to work. I shouldn't have even bothered asking."

"Oh, okay." Birk looked down at their menu, but they had stopped reading it. Their face had fallen, their joy replaced with what looked like disappointment. Mika knew that she had put it there, and she hated herself all the more.

"I'm sorry," Mika said. "I'm not the best company tonight. I wanted this to be perfect, and I'm not doing a very good job of it."

"Perfect is overrated. It's so stuffy and formal. What if we come back here another night and go spend tonight at Rocko's? Maybe being by family will help."

Family. The word hit Mika hard, but she tried not to let it show on her face.

"We are at Rocko's all the time. Tonight is supposed to be special."

"Well, what could be more special than Rocko's? It's where we met, after all."

"Are you sure?" Mika studied Birk, trying to decide if they really wanted to leave. When Birk stood up and tucked in their chair, Mika gave in. She reached into her wallet, pulled out some money for the tip, and stood up.

She grabbed Birk's hand as they walked together to the door.

"Jim is waving us over," Birk said.

Birk was standing right next to Mika, their hands intertwined. The right side of Mika's body felt on fire from the nymph's warmth. Yet she shivered when Birk shouted in her ear. The bar was unusually crowded, with even the aisles between tables full of bodies. A group of brownies had taken over Mika's table. They rarely came to the bar, and Mika had to begrudgingly acknowledge that they hadn't known better than to take her usual spot.

The pair sliced through the crowd with Mika in front, navigating in the small open spaces and moving people out of the way when needed. Birk was right behind her, their hands still joined despite the awkward angle. Even with the room full, Mika could smell wisps of Birk—clean and fresh, just like the forest.

"We were just about to leave, and we thought you two might like a table," Jim said. The couple was sitting against the side wall. *They* had managed to get their usual table.

"It wouldn't do for you to have your first date standing around in that crowd," Dave said.

Mika didn't like the way he looked at them, with a knowing smile and joyful eyes. If it hadn't been for the help the couple had given Birk, Mika would have snapped at both of them. But they seemed to have become adoptive fathers for the nymph.

"Thank you," she managed through clenched teeth.

"Are you sure you are done?" Birk asked.

"Yes," Jim said. "It is much too crowded in here for us old folks. I'm sure you two will appreciate it more."

The men stood up, giving over their chairs and picking up their plates and cups. Mika watched them walk to the side of the bar and deposit the dishes into a plastic tub before making their way to the door.

"That was nice of them," Birk said.

Mika turned her attention back to her date and felt the anger inside her dissipate. Birk nearly radiated with joy. *I will do absolutely anything to keep them happy*, Mika thought.

Birk placed their hands on the table, and Mika reached out, holding them in her own. They sat looking at each other. There was no need for words, just a sappy smile on both of their faces.

"I'm glad that we came here," Birk said.

"Me too," Mika said. But the bar and the noise were all distractions from the person sitting in front of her. Thoughts of their kiss floated in her mind. She stared at Birk's lips, remembering how soft and warm they were. They could abandon the table and just cling to each other, making their own space to dance in the throngs of people.

"It seems everyone thought Rocko's was a great plan for tonight. It looks like it is just Tim and Rocko. They probably won't have time to come around and take orders."

The words sliced into Mika's fantasies, causing her to come back to the moment. "I can go order for us."

"Why don't you save the table, and I'll go up. I want the chance to say hi to Tim anyway."

Mika watched as Birk stood up from the table and made their way through the crowd. No one moved for them, but

Birk had a way of slipping into a space as soon as it opened up, making their journey to the bar an effortless one.

"Interesting that you would choose today, of all days, to finally make your move."

The voice wasn't loud, but the deep baritone was easily heard over the crowd. Mika turned, unsurprised to find Rocko behind her.

"Why do you say that?"

He looked at her, unblinking.

"You already heard," she said. "How could you possibly have heard? It was a private witch matter that only happened a few hours ago."

"Invitations have already started going out to the more prominent witch families."

"Shit. Don't tell Birk, okay? I am going to tonight. I just wanted one date before ..."

"You're going through with it?" Rocko moved to the side of the table so she didn't have to keep twisting to see him. It was considerate, but it also blocked the view of the bar, and Mika found she already missed the nymph.

"I don't know. I don't see how I have much of a choice. Magick requires two opposite forces. If I don't marry, then I will be letting down my entire coven."

"I seem to remember someone else recently finding out that the rules of their world were less specific than they had been told. I don't know much about witch magick, but it seems to me that it doesn't make much sense for it to require such binaries when humans and magickal creatures have never been binary. Unless you have doubts about non-binary identities?"

Mika didn't even bother to respond to him. She just gave him her customary gaze of annoyance until he wandered away. Birk was already headed back from the bar with a bottle of beer and a glass of sparkling water. They dumped the drinks on the table, causing their glass to spill slightly, and then collapsed in their seat.

"When were you going to tell me?" Birk asked.

Mika looked up at the bar and saw Tim staring at them. He shrugged his shoulders slightly as if in apology and then went back to taking orders.

"Don't blame him," Birk said. "Tim figured that I already knew, considering I was with you and everyone else in the magickal community knows. Are you going to marry him?"

"I was told right before our date. I haven't had time to figure anything out. I was going to tell you, I just haven't had the right moment."

"The right moment. Is there a right moment on a date to tell someone that you are engaged? Why would Robert even care? He seems happy enough to keep leading the coven. Why now?"

To the outside community, the coven leader was the ultimate leader of the witches. Mika didn't know why the elders were considered a taboo subject for outsiders. It wasn't something even specifically mentioned, but every witch knew their council was a coven secret. Even now, with everything coming down around her, Mika couldn't bring herself to explain exactly why she had to marry Rob.

"Do you want to marry him?"

"No. I don't want to, and I can assure you he doesn't want to marry me either. Sometimes it doesn't matter what you want. You have to do what your family needs you to. I owe them everything, and this is what they are asking in return."

"Family, real family, isn't conditional."

"I wasn't born into the coven." Mika found she couldn't look directly at Birk as she told her story. She focused on the table, her hands balled into fists before her. "My parents died when I was a baby and I was put into foster care. The coven found me and brought me back as one of their own. They gave me parents and an amazing childhood that I'm not sure

I would have had otherwise. I have been groomed for as long as I can remember to be the next coven leader. I can't walk away now."

"Why not? You have people who love you for who you are—all of who you are. You could come stay with me until you get on your feet, or longer if you want. If that doesn't work, I'm sure Rocko would take you in—he's done it before."

"I can't leave my family." Mika's voice started to rise. "I can't abandon everyone because I can't control a part of myself."

"You do not have to change yourself for them. There is nothing wrong with who you are. Why don't you find a spell or something? Help them to understand, or give you more time."

"That's not how magick works." Mika did yell that time, slamming both her fists on the table.

"It seems to me that you don't know how magick works," Birk said.

Rocko appeared suddenly beside them, his presence causing them both to look up.

"I know you have a lot to talk about, but if you can't calm down, then I am going to have to ask you to do it someplace else."

Mika looked around the bar, realizing that everyone had stopped what they were doing and were now gawking at them.

"I'm sorry," Mika said. "I didn't mean to yell. I'll keep myself under control."

"Are you okay?"

"We're fine," Birk said. "It is just a difficult discussion."

Rocko gave them one last glance and then left.

"I'm sorry," Mika said. "I don't know what to do."

"Don't marry him. Don't give up on us before we have even had a chance."

Mika tried to imagine what it would be like cutting off all ties with Birk and settling in as Rob's wife. A part of her broke inside, and she knew that she could not go through with the marriage.

"They don't understand. If they only knew what I feel for you, then they wouldn't keep pushing this. I know I don't need Rob for magick—I need you."

"Who are *they*?" Birk asked.

"Will you go with me? If they see us together, I think they will understand."

"It's never that simple. You saw what happened with my family."

"Please." Mika stood and extended her hand to Birk. "Come with me."

Birk let out a large sigh before putting their hand in Mika's. "I'm not sure this is the right way forward, but if it is what you want to do, then I will be there beside you."

Mika leaned in, letting her lips settle on the nymph's. They were just as soft and sweet as she remembered them. Then she led them both out of the bar.

Mika didn't even bother to go back to her car. She just started walking the block and a half toward the coven house. The building was unassuming from the outside. Most humans probably thought it was a church, the way it was just one building with a large parking lot and an even larger lawn. During an event, it was full of people flooding the area. Other times, like tonight, it looked abandoned. There were just two cars in an otherwise empty parking lot.

"What are we doing here?"

Instead of responding, Mika walked to the side door and released a small amount of magick so the lock would recognize her presence and open. Inside, the room was dark, with just a trivial light escaping from the door on the stage. Mika walked to it. She could feel Birk following her, trusting her even now.

When they reached the steps of the stage, Mika turned to Birk.

"I need you to stay here. They are not going to be very happy that I brought you, but if you go back with me, it will be too much."

Birk gave a slight nod. Mika paused, not wanting to leave.

She reached out, searching for Birk's hand. When she found it, she gave it a slight squeeze and then turned and headed toward the elders' chambers.

When she opened the door, light flooded out, momentarily blinding her. She waited until her eyes had adjusted and then entered. Mika had been a regular visitor in the elders' quarters growing up, and the space was familiar to her. There were rooms on either side, most currently unoccupied. At the end of the hall was a large meeting space. Inside, Tom and Divinity, the night caretaker, were talking, probably going over the day's events as they switched out. They both turned to look at her when she stepped into the room.

"I need to speak to the elders," Mika said. It came out hesitantly.

"They are asleep right now," Tom said.

Divinity sat quietly, allowing Tom to take control of the situation as head caretaker. She was Black, with her hair currently in braids. Seeing her here was just as awkward as when they were thirteen and had snuck away from a ritual bonfire to practice kissing. The next week, Divinity had shown up at school with a new boyfriend, breaking Mika's heart. They hadn't talked much since. "Please," Mika begged her. "I need to speak to them, it's important."

Tom put his hands on her shoulders and turned her toward the doorway. "It's late. The elders need their sleep. You can come back first thing in the morning after they have rested."

He tried to help her toward the door, causing anger to rise up in Mika. She moved out of his grasp and turned and faced the man.

"I am the next coven leader, and you will show me the respect that is due. Now go and wake the elders. I will meet them in the council chambers."

"I will do no such thing."

"What is all the commotion about?" Elder Sage stood in

the doorway. She was dressed in a silk robe that was tightened around her, only allowing the bottom of her cotton pajamas to peek out. Her hair was wrapped up in a silk scarf, and her feet were covered by pink slippers.

"I'm sorry, Elder." Tom rushed to Elder Sage, about to corral her back to her bedroom in the same way he had done to Mika.

"I need to speak to the council."

Elder Sage held up her hand, causing Tom to stop. "Is it important?"

"It is."

"Very well, the council will see you. Go back to the council room and wait for us there. You two can wake the other elders."

Elder Sage left the room, and Mika waited only a heartbeat before she exited. She could feel Tom's glare on her back the entire time she walked down the hallway. Then she opened the door and flicked on the lights to the council room before leaving the stage and standing next to Birk.

"They are going to see us."

"Who? Who is going to see us?"

Before Mika could answer, the door opened again, and Elder Sage walked onto the stage. Her eyes widened when she saw Birk, and amusement flashed across her face. Behind her was Elder Milton. As usual, he looked half asleep. He seemed to take in Birk's presence without any reaction, just another day of doing what was expected of him.

The door opened again, and Divinity directed Elder Emily to her seat. She wore a long cotton nightgown, and her feet were covered in socks with a grip on the bottom. Divinity saw the nymph and gave a quick, concerned look at Mika before returning to her caretaker duties.

Elder Nam was brought out in her wheelchair. Tom picked her up and transferred her to her seat before placing a blanket over her lap. He took his time carefully tucking it in around the frail frame. Finally, he stood, and the caretakers returned to the elders' quarters. Elder Nam was able to see Birk for the first time.

"Why have you brought her?"

"Elders, Birk's pronouns are they/them," Mika said. "I ask that you please show some respect and use them correctly."

"Respect?" Elder Nam said. "You have brought a non-witch into the coven house and are parading her in front of the elders, and you want us to show respect?"

"It has made for a lively evening," Elder Sage said. "It was getting so boring around here."

Mika felt Birk tugging on her arm, trying to get her attention. "Who are these witches? Why have we come to see them?"

"Yes, why have you woken us up insistent that it was an emergency to show us this nymph?" Elder Nam said.

"If I could please have a moment to explain—"

"Now she wants to explain. Like it isn't obvious why they are here. Isn't it obvious, Milton? They have stars in their eyes."

Elder Milton bobbed his head, seemingly disinterested in what was happening.

"I thought we were going to see Robert," Birk said.

Mika stomped her foot in frustration. She felt like a petulant child, but nothing was happening the way she had planned. No one would stop long enough to listen to her. "This is the elders' council. They give important wisdom to the coven leader. It was them that made the decision that I should marry. And this is Birk, my, well, we've only been on one date, and a disastrous one at that, but I hope one day they will become my partner. So you see, I can't marry Rob because I am not attracted to men."

Elder Nam tried to scoot forward in her seat, but her muscles were too tired and weak, and she ended up just leaning forward. "So you thought you would bring your little *friend* before us and our decision would change? Your relationship was the reason that you are getting married in the first place. I couldn't care less if you are attracted to him. All that matters is that you marry him."

"Why?" Mika asked.

"You know why," Elder Sage said. "You have been instructed in magick since you were a child. I myself have tutored you. This is not a lack of knowledge but a lack of obedience. Do you think I wanted to marry Milton? No, I wanted to marry this gorgeous vampire kin. His skin was so smooth, and his smile made me melt. But the coven came first, and in time, our relationship blossomed. You will do the same because you must. The magick requires it."

Birk grabbed Mika's arm, holding tight. "We should go."

"Go, go, go," Elder Emily said, as if still asleep.

"You should go, child. Leave this one alone; she is not for you," Elder Nam said.

"You don't need to do this," Birk said. "Come with me. I can protect you the same way you protected me."

"Enough," Elder Sage said. "Mika will be staying here. She knows her place and her responsibilities and will not forsake them for you. There is no need to wait for Samhain for the wedding. Given the circumstances, I think it should be moved up."

"Next week," Elder Nam said.

"Next week," Elder Sage said. "It is best that Mika not be allowed around this nymph ever again. In fact, we believe it best that no witches associate with her. Now leave. It is late, and we should be returning to bed."

"No," Birk said. "I understand that you have lived a long life and have learned much, but that does not give you an excuse to close yourself off from the reality of the world. You may believe that the world operates in binaries, but I am right here before you to contradict that. You cannot expect Mika to give up this part of herself because you have decided that it isn't real."

"You dare lecture us on how magick works? I have spent my whole life in its service, and I think I have learned more than you. You can dress up however you like, but that doesn't change who you are."

"You are a disgrace to your family," Elder Nam said. "You abandoned your responsibilities and refused to listen to your mother, all so you could follow some fad. You were tainted by the human-turned-vampire. We will not allow you to taint our coven in turn."

Mika saw the tears welling up in Birk's eyes. Their heart ripped in two when Birk muttered their name. She knew that she should step up and defend Birk against the elders, but they were right. She should have never brought the nymph here. They could not be together because Mika owed the coven everything.

"I'm sorry," she said.

"Come with me," Birk said.

Mika stood frozen, watching as Birk realized that she would not follow them. Even with tears streaming down their face, they held their shoulders high as they turned and walked toward the door. They passed Robert, who must have slipped in during the argument, and gave him a scathing look before walking out the door, leaving Mika for the last time.

"Now that this foolishness is done, we think Mika should return home," Elder Sage said.

"You should stay there until you are called to come before the council again. We will have wedding details to discuss."

Mika didn't know what to say. There were no words left. Their entire lives were crashing down around them, and she didn't know how to pick up the pieces, so she gave up trying.

"I'll walk her home to make sure she arrives safely," Robert said.

"Very well," Elder Nam said. She slipped her hand into

her robe and pulled out the small bell. When she rang it, both Tom and Divinity came and started preparing the elders once again for bed.

"Shall we?" Robert asked.

Mika followed him like a lamb being led to slaughter.

I t only took a few minutes to reach Mika's house. Neither Mika nor Robert had said a word to each other. The night had grown chilly, and Mika wished she hadn't left her jacket in her car, but it would have taken just as long to go back to the car. Besides, Mika felt that she deserved the cold after how she had managed to hurt Birk.

As they approached the yard, Mika grabbed her keys out of her pocket and selected the correct one so that by the time they reached the door, she had it in the lock. She also used her personal energy to unlock the magickal lock she had placed on her door.

"I think we should talk," Robert said.

"There is not much to say. Unless you have a way to stop the wedding."

"Maybe the elders are right. I don't want to give up my position any more than you seem willing to step into the role, but they are getting older. Maybe we are both fighting the inevitable."

"Maybe," Mika said. She opened her door, stepped inside, and closed it before Robert could stop her. She leaned against the doorframe, feeling his energy outside. She waited until it moved away, and then sagged down to the floor.

Mika had left a light on by the front door when she had left, and it illuminated most of the living room. It was simply furnished with a couch and a side chair. There was an end table between them that held another lamp and a book. Her home was plain, with light brown furniture that matched the white walls and brown hardwood floor. At least once a week, Mika would dust and scrub to make sure everything was clean, even though she didn't leave much of an impact behind. The house had served Mika as a refuge since she had moved in over a decade ago. She loved the simplicity, but now, as she looked into the room, it felt boring. Mika couldn't help but wonder what Birk would think of this space if they were to see it. They would most definitely add some plants and some sort of color. Maybe a purple afghan on the back of the couch and some colorful pillows.

But none of that mattered because Birk would never see this place. It would be Rob who would move in, turning this house from a refuge to a constant reminder of what Mika had lost. It would change in small ways, Mika was certain, but neither of them would be comfortable in each other's space.

Mika decided that there was no use dwelling on the inevitable. She picked up the mail that was piled beside her from the slot in the door and walked into the kitchen.

This room was also spotless, mostly because Mika didn't cook. She preferred to take most of her meals out, and those that were eaten at home required very little prep. Mika walked over to the fridge, opened it, and looked inside. It was full of beer, a loaf of bread, and some sandwich fixings. Her stomach grumbled, remembering that they had never gotten to the eating portion of the date, and the thought immediately made Mika lose her appetite. She reached in, grabbed a bottle of beer, and sat at the kitchen table.

Birk would add some plants behind the sink in the window, Mika thought. *They would fill the kitchen with bright towels that serve no purpose except to bring color to the room.* Mika tried to shut off that line of thinking.

She twisted off the top of her beer and took a long swallow. Then she rooted through the mail. Most of it was junk mail addressed to the current resident and trying to sell her things she would never need. But one envelope stood out. It was bright blue and covered in rainbow stickers that sparkled when they hit the light. Mika flipped over the envelope and looked at the return address. It was from the coven in Southern California. This was the first, the only, reply to the letters that she had sent out asking if there was another way of practicing magick. It was a desperate hope. Mika held the envelope in her hands, uncertain if she wanted to open it and read what was inside.

With nothing left to lose, Mika went to her kitchen stationery drawer and pulled out a letter opener. Her hands trembled slightly as she ripped through the blue paper and tugged free a sheet of stationery that was covered in cute cartoon animals. She allowed one moment to ground herself, and started reading.

Mika,

Hi! We were very excited to receive your letter. We don't hear from the more traditional covens all that much. We assume they would rather pretend that we do not exist so they can go about their rules and ceremonies. Honestly, it works well for us. That way, they don't try to force us to carry the same stick up our butt. Anyway, we are glad you reached out.

Your letter was very formal and proper. Thankfully for you, we were able to understand what you were really asking and are more than happy to answer all your questions.

Is magick binary? I assume you didn't mean to ask, "Can you code magick?" You can. We have an amazing computer science witch who writes all their spells in binary code. It doesn't help the rest of us all that much, but it works out well for them.

If you mean gender binaries, well, no. You don't need that at all. All that nonsense was brought over with colonization and all the homophobic views. It bothers all of us here that the traditional families keep spouting that nonsense, but we do what we can, like answering your letter.

Right now, our coven is headed by a member of a polyamorous throuple. They are all feminine. I am going to assume that you are very sheltered and don't know what polyamorous means. Simply, it means that more than two people are in a relation-ship together. The actual relationship dynamics change and I won't go into all the details, but rest assured, it is all consensual and works as well as any relationship.

You didn't ask, but I am going to assume it is because you didn't even think to ask, but no, you do not have to be in a physical relationship to produce magick. I have a theory that this is the traditional family's way of getting their freak on, but then they ruin it by making it all conventional.

As for gay and queer relationships? Yep, we have plenty of those over here. We probably have more than would be typically found because this is California and because our coven takes in a lot of strays. I am a major lesbian and was our last coven leader. I led for a few years and had several magickal partners in that time. I felt the call to move on and gave over the head of the coven to a more magickal witch who joined our fold.

That is another thing. We don't usually serve as coven leaders for decades. We recognize that there are different times and places where we need to lead and others when we need to step down.

I have the approval of the coven to extend an invitation for you to come visit. Don't worry about planning it all out—just pop in when you have time. We don't stand on formality here. I'll drop the address down below.

We can't wait to meet you,

Vi & the SoCal Coven

By the time Mika finished reading, her head was spinning. Never before had she heard witches talk with such informality. They had almost skipped reaching out to the SoCal coven because of their reputation of being troublemakers, and trouble was written all over the letter. They didn't seem to follow any witch traditions. But ... if magick did not require a relationship ... if it didn't require binary gender forces to work ... if any part of what Vi said was true ... then Mika could be with Birk. She wouldn't have to marry Rob.

Mika took one last look around her boring house. She had nothing else to lose at this point. She strode into her bedroom, reached under the bed, pulled out her barely used suitcase, and put it on her properly made bed. Then she went into her dresser and started pulling out pressed shirts, placing them carefully in the suitcase. She went to her closet and chose some of her skirts that would be easiest to travel in. Then, she finished it off with a collection of undergarments and socks. She packed enough for two weeks.

Mika carefully zipped up her suitcase, pulled out a spare jacket, and headed to her front door.

The night was quiet. The witches lived intermixed with the humans of Ember; after all, they were human, too, just with a connection to magick. It was late enough that most of them were tucked up tight in their beds, giving Mika the night to herself, and with it came silence. With the silence came doubt. Mika was not impulsive. She was sensible. She did what was expected of her even when it was not what she wanted to do.

However, every time she thought about turning around, Birk popped into her mind, and then the bright blue envelope with rainbow stickers. If there was a chance, no matter how slim, Mika had to explore it.

It was a short walk to where Mika had parked her car. She had left it near Rocko's, and there were still plenty of other cars around since other magickal creatures tended to be more nocturnal. She opened her trunk and placed her suitcase in the empty hatchback.

"Hiya."

Mika jumped. She turned around, ready to fight off an attack, but pulled her fist back at the last second. Rob stood a few feet away.

"What are you doing here?"

"I could ask you the same thing."

Rob looked a lot like a younger version of his father. He had a lanky frame that was still toned. He also still had a full head of brown hair. But there was the same square chin and squinty eyes.

"Are you going somewhere?" Rob asked.

Mika didn't respond. Instead, she closed the back of her car and walked toward the driver's door.

"Take me with you," Rob said.

"You don't even know where I am going."

"It doesn't matter. Any place is better than here."

Mika opened up the driver's door and slid in. Before she had managed to put on her seatbelt and start the car, Rob had slid into her passenger seat.

"You can't go," Mika said.

"If you kick me out, I will tell the elders that you left."

"No, you won't." Mika checked her rearview mirror and two side mirrors to make sure they were still in the correct positions.

"You're right, I won't. However, I may be quite loud. It will be so loud that people may come and investigate. I'm sure it won't be long before word gets back to my father, and they will go and bring you back."

Mika looked Rob over. He was in a simple T-shirt and jeans. He hadn't even bothered to put on a jacket. He had no bag of any sort.

"What were you doing out here anyway?"

Rob grabbed his seatbelt and put it on. "I was on my way to your house so that we could strategize on how to get out of this wedding. I have been following you since you left."

Mika checked for traffic before pulling out of the parking spot and started heading for the road out of town.

"I didn't realize that your plan would be to run away. Honestly, I didn't think you had it in you. So, where are we going?"

"California." Mika stopped at a stop sign, put on her blinker, and turned onto the highway that would lead to the freeway.

"California? Why are we headed to California?"

Mika checked for any other cars on the road before taking one hand off the wheel and reaching into her pocket. She pulled out the folded envelope and handed it over to Rob. It gave Mika a few minutes of silence while he read and then reread the letter. She kept her eyes on the road, paying careful attention for wildlife springing from the bushes.

"Do you think this is true?" he finally asked.

"I don't know, but if it is, then everything they have ever told us is a lie."

They were quiet, each lost in their thoughts for the next few hours. Mika found the freeway, and they joined the trucks that were driving through the night.

"I heard that you brought your partner to visit the elders. I wished I could have seen that."

"You don't. It was a disaster. I don't know what I was thinking."

"You were thinking that you were in love and would do anything to make them understand. But they are so set in their ways, I don't think they will ever look outside the views they've grown up with."

Mika turned on her blinker and then slowly moved over to the left lane. She made sure to keep to the speed limit as she passed a semi, giving it plenty of space before she put her blinker back on and switched to the right lane.

"I'm sorry," she said.

"Why are you sorry?"

"I'm sorry that I don't want to marry you."

"You have nothing to be sorry for. I don't want to marry you either."

They passed billboards with fast-food advertisements, and Mika's stomach began to growl.

"You're the only one who doesn't want something from me," Rob said. "My parents want grandchildren. The coven wants to partner me off for the greater good. Every unmarried witch wants me to give them a forbidden love story. I think even some of the married ones want that. I know where I stand with you. You want someone else, and I find that refreshing."

"I care about you," Mika said.

"Just not in a romantic way."

"Yes. I'm sorry. I don't want to hurt you. You're my best friend."

Mika turned her head briefly to look at Rob. He was staring out the front window, face pinched in concentration.

"I don't want you to be sorry. I don't want anyone to be sorry. I want it to be okay. I want to be able to have wonderful, glorious friendships, and maybe some friends with benefits, and have that be enough. I don't think I am meant to ever be in a relationship."

Mika passed the exit for the fast-food restaurant and kept on driving. They still had over twelve hours before they would make it to the coast; there would be plenty of time to get food.

The sun had only been up for a few hours when Mika pulled off to get gas. Rob had fallen asleep right after their last talk and hadn't stirred. She had been hesitant to leave him alone to go grab food, so she had stayed on the road, continuing on their journey. The hunger had been the only thing keeping her awake when the anxiety of leaving her home had passed. They were nearly there, and while it wasn't too late to turn back, Mika found a sense of freedom coursing through her veins.

As she pulled up to a gas pump, Rob finally began to stir.

"Morning," Mika said.

"I didn't mean to fall asleep on you. I should have helped you stay awake."

"I would have woken you up if I had needed you."

Rob stretched his arms and then opened his door. Mika opened hers, enjoying the sensation of standing after the hours unmoving in the car. Her stomach let out a loud rumble in protest at being ignored.

"I'll go grab us some food while you fill up," Rob said.

It didn't take long before Mika's car was full. It didn't have a large tank, but it made up for it with excellent gas mileage aided by some magick. With as little as Mika drove, she could usually go a year or more before needing a new tank, but now they had made it a little over six hundred miles. It was frivolous magick that was only approved because it helped the environment. Mika waited anxiously for the spell to start to wear off just so she could set it again. It was one of the most complicated things she was allowed to do outside of the solstice ceremonies.

Mika moved the car to an empty parking space and went inside to use the restroom and enjoy the sensation of movement. Rob had picked them up some breakfast burgers from the fast-food joint inside the gas station, and Mika added a few snacks for the rest of the trip. They wouldn't need to stop again until they reached California.

"I think you should let me drive the rest of the way," Rob said.

"I'm fine. I just need some food, and I will be good to go."

"Once that food hits your system, you are going to pass out. You have been driving for eight hours. It's my turn now."

"It's my car." Mika walked over to the driver's door, but Rob got there first, putting his body between hers and the door.

"Let me drive," he said.

Mika stood there staring at him, doing her best to look

upset, but mostly, her mind was on the greasy food in the bag in his hands.

"The sooner you relent, the faster you will get to eat. You know that you can trust me. I will be good to your car and will keep her at the speed limit the entire time."

"You will use the blinker?" Mika asked.

"I will use the blinker and follow every traffic law."

"You promise?"

"Promise. Now give me the keys."

Mika relented, pulling out the keys from her pocket and exchanging them for the bag of food. She went over to the passenger door and hesitated before going inside. She didn't eat in her car, ever. But she also had never taken it on a road trip, and the gas station did not offer much space to eat. Mika finally decided that if she could hand over the keys to her car, she could find it in herself to eat in it, also.

Once she sat down, she pulled out the food and passed half of it over to Rob. "Do not spill."

"I wouldn't dream of it. And if, by some small chance, I do spill, I promise that I will clean it up."

"I suppose that is good enough."

Mika took a large bite of her burger, moaning in delight. Once the sandwich was finished, she felt her eyes start to close, and before Rob had left the gas station parking lot, she had drifted off to sleep.

The sun was still bright in the sky when they pulled up to the address in the letter.

"Do you think this is it?" Mika asked.

The building was a large square surrounded by windows. In the front, there was a small gate that they could not see over because of all the cars blocking their view. The area was clean, but the paint was flaking off. It had seen better days. There was no sign or indication that witches were nearby, but even the coven house in Ember was discrete, and they were surrounded by the magickal community.

"There is only one way to find out. Let's find a place to park and go see what's there."

They drove down the block, looking for a place to pull in. There were cars everywhere. They were parked so close that, in some areas, they were touching each other. Some cars parked up on sidewalks, making it inaccessible to walk around them, especially for someone who had assisted mobility.

Eventually, they found a spot a few blocks away that Rob was able to pull into because of the hatchback's small size. There was no parallel parking in Ember, and it took a few tries before he was able to fit the car into the spot. They both got out, slightly frazzled.

Mika looked at her suitcase alone in the car. They didn't know where they were going, and bringing it felt premature, but at the same time, her car was alone and far from their goal.

"Just bring it," Rob said. "If you leave it behind, you will just continue worrying about it."

So they walked back to the address, trying to avoid the cars parked on the sidewalks, and trailing a suitcase behind them.

Even though they only saw a few people sitting out on their front steps, there were radios playing and TVs blaring. Everything seemed so close together. You could barely walk between buildings, and most were apartments. With so many people, it was no wonder there was no place to park.

It seemed to take forever before they made it to the gate of the unmarked building. Mika could not hear anything past the gate, but she sensed the magick keeping the building from prying eyes. She glanced at Rob to see if he could feel it as well.

"At least we know we are in the right place," he said.

Mika centered herself and then pushed the gate open.

It only took one step past the barrier before they entered an entirely new world. They arrived in a courtyard surrounded on all sides by colorful apartments. Each unit was painted anything from bright pink to tan. In the center of the apartments was some fake grass covered in lounge chairs and outdoor plastic picnic sets. There was also what looked like an outdoor kitchen that had a group of people gathered around it.

At the sound of the gate clicking shut, the group turned and looked at them. There was silence before one individual broke away.

"You're here. You must be Mika, right? I expected you to

come but not quite so fast. Not that it is any problem. Not at all—it's exciting. I'm Vi, and my pronouns are she/her."

Vi was shorter at just over five feet tall. Her hair was blonde and cropped close to her head. Despite it being fall, she was wearing a tie-dye T-shirt, short jean shorts, and nothing else. Even her feet were completely bare. Mika suddenly felt overdressed and, with her jacket still on, very hot.

Vi circled them, looking them up and down, reminding Mika of the pixies in the bar. Maybe she had a distant pixie relative, if that was even a possible thing.

"I'm Rob. This is Mika."

"Interesting," Vi said. Then she went back to ignoring Rob. "Welcome. You can put your suitcase anywhere and make yourself comfortable. We were just getting dinner started, so you have perfect timing. Let me introduce you."

Vi grabbed Mika's suitcase and then her hand. Mika was so startled that she didn't even have time to protest before she was whisked away to the kitchen area, where Vi let go of Mika's hand only to hold up her own as if waiting for something. Mika looked at it in confusion.

"Coat. It's still 70 degrees out here; you won't need that for a while."

Mika took off her coat and handed it to the woman, watching as she moved everything she had brought off to the corner of the courtyard.

"Don't worry. No one will touch anything."

Mika turned toward the voice and saw a young girl dressed up in an apron and holding one of those large outdoor spatulas. In front of her was a large grill covered in at least a dozen burgers and another dozen hot dogs.

"That's Zim," Vi said. "She is our resident cook when she is not doing homework."

"I would much rather be cooking."

"Which is why you do your homework."

It seemed like a routine that they had done over and over again.

"Are you her mother?" Mika asked.

They both started laughing, and Mika was uncertain what she had said wrong.

"I found Zim hitchhiking about a year ago and brought her back to our coven. Her parents kicked her out when they found her kissing another girl. I'm not her mom, but we are her family."

Mika looked at the teenager and then at Vi. Neither seemed overly concerned about this topic, even though Mika personally knew the pain that must have come from being rejected for a part of who she was.

"Are you … Do you like …" Mika tried to find a way to ask but did not want to insult their host.

"Do I like other women?" Vi said. "Yep, I like them very much. My family wasn't too thrilled either. They didn't kick me out, but they made it very clear that it was in my best interest to find somewhere else to be when I graduated from high school. I ended up here also and have been here for ten years now."

"Except she is leaving us," Zim said.

Mika looked up in interest at this.

"I told you, kid, I'm not sure what is next for me. I just know there is something else for me to be doing, another part of my journey. Even if it does take me away from here, it doesn't mean I still won't be family and be there for you when you need me."

Zim turned away from the women and started focusing back on the grill.

"This here is Greg and Frank."

Two men were sitting at a table next to the kitchen. They were holding hands and talking but looked up when their names were called. They each gave a tiny wave and went back to their conversation.

"Greg was born here. Honestly, one of the few who was born into the coven instead of finding us. Frank is his husband. He isn't a witch, but we claim him all the same."

"It's funny watching him try and do magick," Zim chuckled.

Mika looked up to find Rob and saw that he was still standing near the gate, watching everything unfold. She motioned for him to join them. He scanned the gathering and then haltingly walked forward.

"Is this your soon-to-be husband?" Vi asked.

Mika looked at her, startled. She didn't remember mentioning anything about Rob in her letter, and she hadn't even known about the wedding at the time.

"We aren't as cut off from the families as they would have you believe. We actually may have more information than most, considering how many have come from the other families."

"You knew about me before I wrote to you?"

"We knew you existed and that you hadn't been given charge of the coven. There was speculation as to why, but no one knew for certain. At least until your letter arrived."

"Well, that smells good."

Mika turned to the new voice that emerged from one of the apartments. The person paused to take in Mika and Rob and then walked up to both of them.

"River. Ze/Zir. Nice to meet some new faces."

"Mika." Then, after a pause, she added, "she/her."

"Rob. He/Him. Nice to meet you also."

"You two a couple?" River asked.

"No," Rob said. "We are supposed to be, but it didn't work out that way for either of us."

River stared at them expectantly, and Rob continued.

"Mika likes women, and while I like people well enough, I wouldn't want to marry or date any of them."

"You and me both," River said, patting Rob on the shoulder and then turning zir attention to the food.

The courtyard began to fill with people. Rob wandered off to talk to River, and Vi had left to talk to some of the new arrivals. Mika found herself alone and unsure of what to do. She sat down at one of the plastic tables and watched. People would come home from work and make their way to the food to eat. Others would grab some food before heading out for the night. At least half a dozen kids were running around playing with each other while the adults all looked after them.

What was most mystical to Mika was seeing women and men openly affectionate with each other. There was even a group of three women that Mika was sure were in a relationship, and she couldn't help but wonder if one of them was the new coven leader.

"Not everyone is gay." Mika jumped when Zim talked. "But enough are that it is normal here. You can just be yourself."

She put down a plate with a burger, a salad, and some chips.

"You are supposed to serve yourself, but I know how awkward that can be when you are new. I hope that you eat meat. If not, I have some veggie burgers coming up."

"Meat's good," Mika said, but Zim had already moved back to the grill.

After everyone had eaten, those who stayed outside gathered together around a metal fire pit surrounded by chairs. Mika hesitated at first and then stood up and joined them. She felt more comfortable when she saw Rob there still talking to River.

"I think the new person should light the fire," Zim said.

"Alright, you are up," Vi said. The woman had ignored Mika since she had talked to Rob, but now she seemed to be giving Mika her full attention.

"Okay," Mika said, looking around. "Where are the matches?"

The whole group laughed as if Mika had told a joke, and she blinked uncertainly.

"You light it with magick," Zim said.

"Magick? But that would be frivolous."

The group had stopped laughing and now looked as if she had insulted them all.

"I mean, it is against the rules to use magick on something as small as a fire. Magick is only supposed to be used around sabbats or for some extenuating situations."

"You have never started a fire with magick?" Zim asked. "But you have so much of it. It's easy. Here, let me show you."

Zim squinted her eyes in concentration and pointed her finger at the fire pit. After a few seconds, a small flame seemed to jump from her finger, where it settled along the logs before beginning to spread.

"Close your eyes," Vi said. "Seriously, close your eyes."

Mika sighed and then closed her eyes.

"Feel the air around you. It is full of magick ready to be used."

Mika could feel the magick. She could always feel the magick. She had just been taught to tune it out, to pretend it didn't exist unless it was a ritual and she was pulling it from others, but it was always around her, calling her and begging her to use it.

"Now feel the fire. There is a flame there waiting for you. Can you feel it?"

Mika nodded. The fire was right there, dancing with its own power.

"Feed some of the magick into the fire. Make the flames go higher."

Mika fed her power into the fire and then opened her eyes when she felt the intense heat. The fire was shooting up past the second-floor apartments and had escaped the fire pit on every side. People were scrambling, running away from the flames. Several of them came back with fire extinguishers, spraying them on the fire like it was not their first time.

"Let it go," Vi said.

Mika realized that she had still been feeding magick into the fire. She reluctantly released it, and the flames began to drop and eventually were extinguished.

"I'm sorry," Mika said. She expected to be told to grab her suitcase and leave. There was a reason magick was only used during rituals, and she had just proven why. Instead, she realized that the group was laughing. They sat back down, the fire extinguishers at their sides.

"Well, I don't think anyone will ever be able to top that," one of the people said.

Then the voices went off, telling stories about past trainings and previous fires, but Mika couldn't help the shame of losing control. She went and sat down at one of the plastic tables away from the group.

"That isn't on you," Vi said. "Your coven should have trained you better."

"I have been in training since I could walk," Mika said.

"They have trained you to restrain your magick and to only use what was siphoned off of others. They honestly believe that is the only way, but magick is all around us. It makes up every part of the universe. It isn't finite, needing to be conserved for rituals. It is with us, always ready to be used as long as it is respected. This time, don't close your eyes. Look at the tip of your finger and think about the feel of the fire. Only focus on that feeling and pull out the smallest amount possible and put it on the tip of your finger."

Mika felt for the energy of the fire and tempered down the magick—that was something she was used to doing. But then she let out a small amount and watched a flame grow, hovering over the tip of her finger.

"Very good," Vi said. "It usually takes people much longer."

When Mika woke up the next morning, it took her a moment to remember Vi leading her and Rob to one of the residences and handing them each a key. They had opened the door to find a one-bedroom apartment. The living area had a couch and a few chairs, and the bedroom was full of bunk beds. They had each taken one of the bottom bunks and fallen asleep.

Except, the room was empty. Rob was nowhere to be found.

Mika opened her suitcase, pulled out a new outfit, and went into the bathroom to take a shower. It was fully stocked with tiny shampoo bottles, toothbrushes, and even a pile of clean towels. The place seemed to function more as a hotel or hostel than an apartment, and Mika couldn't help wondering how many strays the coven took in to have everything constantly set up for them.

Once she was clean, Mika felt better. It was one thing she could control in what had been a week completely out of her control. Outside in the kitchen area, there were containers of cereal and a selection of milk products put out in ice chests. Rob was sitting talking with River, an empty bowl already in front of him. Mika walked over and started to pour herself some food when she felt Vi come up behind her.

"We don't eat as well on the days that Zim has school. As a reward, Martha tries to cook with her on the weekend and make some muffins or other pastries, but by the time we get to Friday, we are usually back to cereal."

"Does she cook for everyone?"

"We all help out when we can, but cooking is the only thing that motivates her to focus on school, so we let her take charge of it as long as her grades are good. Everyone here contributes something, even if that something is donated to the fund to keep this all going."

"The entire coven lives here?"

Mika took her bowl and started to head toward Rob, but he looked so engaged that she pivoted and went to an empty table.

"No," Vi said. "Staying here is a choice. A lot of us stay because it is the only way that we can afford rent. The coven owned this building long before prices got so out of control. The elders live in another building close to here. We go see them often, and sometimes they come here for a meal, but they mostly prefer where it is quieter."

Mika froze at the mention of the elders, the spoon held in the air above her bowl. Vi looked confused at her alarm and then seemed to understand.

"They don't tell us what to do. We seek their counsel and make sure they are taken care of, but no one would ever force someone to do something against their will, especially not marriage."

Mika dropped the spoon in the bowl, her appetite gone. "They taught me that magick is binary. I couldn't do it alone. I would always need Rob by my side, a partner of the opposite gender."

"Opposite? Do they think gender is a coin that they can toss and get one or the other? Gender is so much more and so much less at the same time. And they conflate it with biological sex like intersex people don't exist. Like there are not as many intersex folks as there are redheads."

"There are?"

"Eat up. I want to show you something."

Mika sat in the passenger seat of Vi's jeep. The top was down, and the wind blew her hair all around. Her hand was firmly clasped on the pole that the door attached to. Just as soon as Vi would speed up, traffic would instantaneously slow down, causing everyone to slam on their brakes. Even when it was almost completely stopped, other cars found a way to move in front of theirs, creating space where there was none. There were so many cars everywhere, and even more people. Mika had never heard so many horns honking in her entire life. By the time they pulled into a parking lot, Mika was ready to never get in a car again. Vi, however, seemed perfectly fine, as if that had been a normal experience.

"We're here," Vi said.

Mika looked around. All she saw were cars and a parking lot full of sand. Vi must have seen her skepticism because she grabbed her hand and started pulling her toward the parking lot until they stood on a sidewalk, also covered in sand, and stared out at even more sand. Beyond that was the ocean, its blue waves lapping lazily against the beach. It would almost have been peaceful if the sand hadn't been full of a few hundred people all setting up their temporary settlements.

Mika grabbed her hand and pulled her until they made it to the wet part of the beach. Vi had slipped off her shoes and was holding them in one hand. They were thin sandals that would have done little to protect from the sand anyway. Mika was wearing her boots. Up until now, they had served her well in every situation. They didn't seem to be faring well, however, as they sunk into the wet sand. But the thought of taking them off and feeling the sand under her toes was too much, so she left them on.

"Is this your first time seeing the ocean? Isn't it glorious? Okay, now I want you to feel the water and see how much of it you can move."

"I think we learned how much of a bad idea that was yesterday."

"Most people have one main element they control. I think it is fair to say that fire is yours."

Mika glared at her and then focused her attention toward the ocean. She tried to think about the waves moving back and forth and their connection to the pull of the moon. Then she reached out, willing more of the water to make its way to the shore.

She realized that there was a problem when people around her started to scream. They were snatching their things and racing away from the water. Vi grabbed her and tried to tug her back, but Mika stood in awe at the waves rushing their way. They had to be at least four stories high. She let the magick go, expecting it to dissipate like the fire had. Except it kept coming.

"What did I do?" Mika asked.

Instead of answering, Vi pulled her farther back. They reached the boardwalk as the wave made landfall. It had shortened some before it came but still ended up spraying them and dragging out some of the towels and chairs into the ocean.

"That was the freakiest thing ever," someone said, before going to collect their remaining belongings and heading to their car.

"I thought it wasn't going to be as strong," Mika said.

"Maybe I should stop underestimating you. No more major magick unless we have something worthy to focus it on. Instead, why don't you try collecting a single drop and bringing it to you."

It seemed like an impossible task, but Mika closed her eyes and focused on the feel of the ocean. It was all one fluid body. There were no drops to call to her, so she finally made her own, causing a small amount of water to ball up and head over. She opened her eyes to see a sideways raindrop land in her hand.

"Fantastic," Vi said.

They headed toward the pier, and Mika was surprised to see that there was a mini carnival set up along the boardwalk, complete with a Ferris wheel and arcade games.

"We can go on it if you want."

Mika eyed the contraption, studying the slim metal polls and the aging seats, and declined. Instead, they headed over toward the arcade games. Vi paid for them to both knock down some metal milk jugs. She went first, and Mika saw her use wind to cause them to drop when her ball missed.

"I must just be lucky," she said.

Mika focused on the ball, causing the wind to drag it exactly where she wanted it to go, and when one of the bottom bottles still didn't drop, she pulled on magick and helped it on its way. They walked away laughing at the attendant's bafflement at what had happened, as well as their rejection of their prizes.

"If magick can be used for everything," Mika said, "what is to stop people from using it with ill intent?"

"Their intent is what stops them. Whatever you put into the universe comes back to you. I'm not saying people deserve what happens if someone hurts them, I am saying the people who do the hurting do not find joy or happiness in their actions, just more misery. Magick is like that. Now, if I were to use magick to help someone, then that intent would come back to me as well. Do you see that?" Vi pointed to a man who was talking to a woman who was not happy with the conversation. She kept trying to walk away from him, and he kept getting in her way, stopping her. Vi gave a small smile, and suddenly, the man tripped. The women took advantage of the situation and ran away.

"You could say that it is never right to use magick to hurt someone, but sometimes you need to do exactly that. You have to assess the situation and use your best judgment."

By the time they made it back to the apartment complex, both women were exhausted. Mika went back and took a shower, washed all the sand off, switched into clean clothes, and then joined Vi in her apartment for dessert.

"Don't you have to work?" Mika asked.

"I'm kind of in a transitionary period."

"You're leaving?"

"I'm meant to be someplace else. Everything in my life ended, and the universe just seemed to be calling me to a new place. I'm just not sure where yet."

They sat down on a plush couch covered in cushions. It was exactly what Mika needed after a long day in the sun.

"I may have been sleeping with my boss, and when her husband found out, it didn't go very well. I know how it sounds, but she neglected to mention she had a husband to me. When the relationship ended, so did my job. It's okay, though, I was never meant to work in an office. I only stayed because the sex was so great."

Mika was speechless. Thankfully, Vi did not need her to participate in any of the conversation.

"When we received your letter, I thought, *This is it. This is where I am supposed to be next.*" Vi moved closer, and before Mika knew what was happening, she leaned forward, about to connect their lips.

Mika stood up, dropping her ice cream bowl on the carpet.

"I'm sorry." Mika went to pick up the bowl and then saw Vi. She turned around and raced toward the door, not stopping until she made it to her temporary home. Mika unlocked the door and slid down, catching her breath. Visions of the hurt on Birk's face filled her, and she started to cry.

Later, when she was lying in bed pretending to be asleep, she heard the door open. She peeked through the covers, careful not to give away that she was awake, and was relieved to find that it was Rob. He slipped off his shoes, slid into his bunk, and went straight to sleep.

Mika kept her eyes closed as Rob got ready for the day. She hid under her covers, waiting for him to call out her cowardice, but he only briefly glanced in her direction before he left the room. She couldn't help the annoyance that crept up at his lack of interest, but she tried her hardest to stuff it back down. Rob had lived in her shadow since they had been toddlers. Here, he was starting over, and it appeared to be doing him some good. Mika had never seen him so interested in anything. His funk had gotten so bad in Ember that whenever Mika searched him out, she knew to look in his bed; he was always there.

Now, she was the one stuck in bed.

The memory of last night haunted her, filling her with shame. Sure, she hadn't done anything. Mika had left before anything could happen. She hadn't even wanted anything to happen. In the past, she would have been all over the pixie-like witch, but now all she wanted was Birk. Even if they couldn't be together, Mika was not going to betray them.

The bed was not particularly comfortable, and the gnawing of her stomach propelled her out of bed to look through the kitchen cupboards. They were empty. There were not even dishes set inside. Mika had to grudgingly admit that it made sense when newcomers could eat communally, but it did not help her any.

Outside the door, people were laughing and talking as they lingered over their plates. It reminded Mika that it was a weekend. Zim was probably out there cooking right now, and if Mika stayed inside any longer, she would miss out on all of it. She paused and considered her desire for food over the horror of running into Vi. With a loud rumble, Mika's stomach made the final decision.

She hurried and slipped into some new clothes and paused at the door, looking through the peephole. She couldn't see Vi, but then she couldn't see much of anything. Slowly, she cracked open the door and took a look around. No Vi.

Mika made a dash from the door over to Zim. There were trays laid out with picked-over eggs and pancakes. There was even a collection of bacon and sausage.

"There you are," Zim said, turning away from the stove where she was cleaning off the remnants of food. "I was worried you were going to sleep through breakfast. I'm glad there's some left."

"Yesterday was a long day. I ended up sleeping in."

"I heard that you drenched the entire beach. I wish I could have seen that, but I had to go to school." She made a face and went back to cleaning up.

Mika made up a plate of food, settling for vegan sausage when she realized that was all that was left, and thought about taking it back into her room. She could spend the day hiding out and not learning about magick. Except learning was how she was going to get back to Birk, so she looked at the table of people and walked over to join them.

"Do you mind?"

"Go right ahead. I've been meaning to say hi. I'm Martha, she/her, and this is my wife Beth and my other wife Don, both she/her."

Mika sat down at the last open chair and started cutting up her pancakes. "You're the coven leader, correct?"

"I am. I am also fairly new at magick in general, so if you have any advice, I would love for you to share."

"You're new to magick?" Mika realized she had talked with her mouth full and quickly put her hand over her lips, taking the time to compose herself.

"We arrived about six months ago looking for an environment that would be a bit more accepting of our relationship. One of the coven members works for a rental agency and realized that Beth and I were witches, and we ended up here. A few months later, Vi stepped down as coven leader, and as the next powerful, I stepped into the role. Is that not how things are done in your coven?"

"No, not exactly." Mika had eaten most of her food while Martha talked, a bit faster than she normally would have to help hide her bafflement at every new word that left the coven leader's mouth. "Most everyone in our coven is born in. Only rarely do people join from outside, and usually, it is because they were sought out. I'm one of them. There were not any powerful female users of my generation, so they found me when I was an infant and brought me back to the coven. I have been training to become a coven leader for as long as I can remember."

The table sat in silence for a few moments, and Mika tried to ignore the awkwardness of it by finishing the rest of her food.

"So, if you have been training that long, how come you aren't the coven leader already?" Zim asked. She had walked over to listen, a dirty spatula still in her hand.

"Well," Mika hesitated, and thinking about all this high schooler had been through, decided to go for complete honesty. "My coven taught me magick was binary. Magick could only be wielded by a married man and woman for it to work. I'm supposed to marry Rob."

"But you like girls," Zim said.

"I like people who are not men," Mika said. "I am dating … Well, it's complicated, but there is a person back home who I tried to introduce to the elders, and it didn't go very well. I think they must hate me now."

"That is why you have to go back," Vi said.

Mika turned around, surprised that the woman had snuck up behind them—she was usually so loud and full of presence.

"I have to return to serve my family, but I don't want to go back until I know how to convince them that Birk and I can be together. I know they are wrong about magick."

"They probably know it, too. It makes them hold on to their bigoted beliefs all the more. If you are finished, we should probably do some more training."

Mika looked around, uncertain of what to do. Vi may not be the current coven leader, but she appeared to be the most experienced. If Mika was going to learn, then it seemed it would have to be with her. Thoughts of the almost-kiss flashed in her mind, reminding her of the way Birk's lips felt on her own. To buy some time, Mika stood up and went to clean off her plate. Then she picked up a discarded rag and started wiping down the kitchen area.

"I'm sorry about last night," Vi said. "I know I am supposed to be somewhere else, and I thought that somewhere was with you. That doesn't excuse my actions or why I didn't talk to you first. I just wanted you to know that I understand, and I will respect your boundaries from now on."

"I can't do anything else to hurt Birk. They have already been through so much. *I* have put them through so much."

"I understand. I promise completely platonic friendship and nothing else."

Mika looked at the earnest expression on the woman's face and then let out a deep sigh. She had made enough mistakes in the last week; she could forgive this witch for last night.

"Thank you," Mika said. Then she walked toward Vi's apartment and followed her into the house to train.

"This morning, we are going to work on intention magick."

Mika sat in a small room surrounded by five candles laid out in a circle around her.

"I want you to think about something that you want to come to pass, something you strongly desire. When you have that image in your mind, I want you to light the candles—with magick, just so we are clear—invoking the appropriate element. Once you have done air, fire, water, and earth, invoke the candle for spirit and keep that image in your mind as the candles burn. You can wait until the candles extinguish, or if you are confident your intention has set, you can put out the flames."

"You want me to do what?"

Vi frowned. "Do I need to repeat it all?"

"No, I understand the tasks, but magick should never be used for your own desire. It only should be used to help the community."

"Don't worry. I have an idea about that, but right now, I want you to think about yourself. Send your own needs out into the universe. Unless you plan on causing someone harm, the universe will be just fine with this."

Mika hesitated, unsure if this was something she should be doing. Then she thought back to her date with Birk. They had told her to find some magick to fix this situation and how maybe they didn't understand how magick worked. Mika realized that the nymph had been right all along, and she had been too stubborn to listen.

So she pictured herself dancing with Birk. They were happy and together openly, where all of Ember could see them. With that image in her head, she invoked each of the candles, inviting in the elements to help send her image back to the universe. She could feel the magick surrounding her and felt more at peace than she ever had.

When Mika finally opened her eyes, the room was empty, and the candles were flickering, their last bit of flame dancing around before each one extinguished itself. Some part of her knew that everything was going to end up working out even if they couldn't yet see how she was going to manage that.

With the candles secure and double-checked to make sure that there were no lit embers, Mika headed outside. Lunch was in full swing with a large group of people, many of whom Mika had never seen. Mika looked around for Vi but couldn't find her. She did find Rob. Frank was getting up from his table, leaving Rob alone with an empty plate. Mika rushed over and put her hand on Rob's shoulder.

"Don't move. Let me get some food, and then we can talk."

With as absent as he had been, Mika wasted no time picking up a premade sandwich and a bag of chips before walking back over to her fiancé.

"Hi," she said.

"Hi."

"You seem to be doing good here."

His whole face lit up. "I am. Things are different here."

"No one expects anything of you."

"Not just that—they understand. Do you remember River?"

Mika nodded her head as she took a bite of her sandwich.

"Ze was explaining some things to me. River identifies as asexual and aromantic."

"What's that?" Mika asked before taking another bite.

"I still don't understand it all, but basically, River is asexual, meaning ze isn't interested in being physically intimate with anyone. Ze is also aromantic, which means that River isn't interested in being in a romantic relationship with anyone either. There is more to it, and of course, everyone who is asexual or aromantic is a bit different."

"Are you asexual and aromantic?"

"I'm not asexual. I enjoy that well enough. It was always everything else I wasn't comfortable with. I think I am aromantic."

"That is fantastic. I feel like there is so much I still have to learn, but I am so happy that you were able to find some of what you were looking for here."

"There is more." Rob hesitated, as if afraid to continue.

Mika kept eating, giving him his space until he was ready.

"I've been talking to Frank. He works as a computer programmer, and I think it could be something I would be good at. I want to go back to school and get a degree. Here."

"You want to stay?" Mika put down the rest of her sand-wich and let herself process this information. It wasn't too surprising. Rob didn't enjoy Ember, and California had already given him so much more than he'd had. Plus, it was a fantastic community that she knew would support him. "I think that's great."

"You do?" He sat up, his whole body relaxing.

"I do. I have to go back, though."

"I know."

When night fell, Vi led Mika to the center of the group. The courtyard was crowded with more members than just those who lived in the apartment. Vi stood up on one of the plastic chairs, and Mika couldn't help reaching out, expecting it to crumple, but it held steady.

"You all know that I am no longer your coven leader. Martha is doing an excellent job in that role, but tonight, she is letting someone else lead our ritual. We have a visitor from the coven in Ember. She has been with us for a few days, learning about our more colorful version of magick. Tonight, she is going to use me as her second.

"Our neighbors have approached us about recent auto thefts in the area. One home has even been burglarized. Tonight, we will put in the work to help our neighbors and cast a protection spell for our community. Thank you all for being here."

Mika looked at Vi in horror. She didn't know how to do this. She had never practiced the words for this. It wasn't even a proper sabbat.

"Think about this morning," Vi said. "All you need is intention. You already know how to siphon magick and put it toward a cause—now you are just changing the cause."

Vi handed Mika a printed map of the local area. There were roads and basic outlines of buildings, and in blue pen, Vi had written, *We are here.*

Mika closed her eyes, picturing the map. She remembered the buildings they had passed over the last few days. They were apartment buildings, most a few floors with stoops out in front. There were windows that bridged the outside to the families living inside. The map began to transform into an organic place inside Mika's mind. She couldn't see the people, but she could feel them living their lives. They wanted to feel safe, and tonight, the California coven had gathered to give them that.

Mika held on to Vi's hands, feeling the energy that coursed through her, extending it out to feel the energy around her from this community that had accepted her as one of their own for tonight. Then, she took that energy and focused it on the community, visualizing a protective barrier that would keep out those who wanted to cause harm. More magick than she had ever felt coursed through her body, and the distance was farther than any magick she had tried before, but she held on, knowing the people around her were there to support and lend their energy. She did it without words and pomp or ceremony, but she knew the moment that it had been done. Their energy had been sent into the world to help.

When Mika opened her eyes, everyone around her cheered, and the sound vibrated deep into her core. Then some music was put on, and some food and drinks laid out, and a party started that lasted long into the night. Mika, however, moved away from it all, sitting quietly by herself.

Only Vi approached her, and only for a few moments. "You did it, and you didn't need a husband after all." Then she danced away into the arms of the party.

Mika felt lighter. It could have been due to finally completing a ritual, or maybe the people sitting all around her.

"I think Birk would enjoy meeting you all."

The people at the breakfast table didn't miss a beat at Mika's random declaration.

"We would enjoy meeting them as well," Frank said. "When you get everything squared away, bring them by to say hi."

"Or maybe we should all drive to Ember and meet the coven. I've heard magick under a nexus is amazing." The speaker was probably in their mid-twenties and had short black hair. Mika hadn't seen them before, but there were a lot of new faces of people who had slept over.

"Well, wait until I am coven leader, at least. We can't have them kicking me out before I am ordained."

This caused the table to laugh before going back to their previous conversations.

Mika heard the gate open, but people had been going back and forth all morning and she didn't think anything of it until Martha grabbed her shoulder, pushing until she stood up.

"You need to go, now."

She dragged her the short distance to Vi's apartment, not even asking before opening the door and pushing her inside. A few seconds later, the door opened again, and Rob fell in.

"What was that about?" Mika said.

Rob put his finger to his lips and whispered, "My dad's outside."

Mika pushed past him and went to the peephole in the door, but all she could see were the backs of everyone standing up facing the gate. So, she reached for the doorknob. Rob's hands covered her own, and they had a silent conversation that only two people who were raised together could have.

Don't open it, Rob's eyes pleaded.

I don't let other people fight my battles, Mika glared.

"We could just crack the door and find out what is going on before we rush out there," Rob said.

Mika gave a curt nod and then gently opened the door a crack. It was just enough for them to see and hear what was happening and not enough for someone to see them.

"We know they are here," Robert said.

"You keep saying that," Martha said. "What you aren't telling us is who you are looking for. As you can see, we have a lot of people here."

"I told you we are looking for two of our coven members. We are here to bring them home."

Mika knew that tone of voice and could picture Robert's cheeks flaring red in frustration. It was a new experience seeing someone else making him so upset.

"Do you know who they came with? Maybe they are asleep on someone's couch. I'm sure we can look around for them if you just give us some idea of who you want."

"What's going on?" A hand grabbed Mika's shoulder, and she had to stop the squeal that would give away their location.

"They found us," Mika said, once her heart had stopped pounding.

Vi pushed between Mika and the door, allowing her to see through the crack.

"Don't worry; we are good at this. Everyone thinks we are misfits and airheads, and we can play into their expectations until they give up and go home."

"My dad isn't the type to give up."

Vi shrugged, and they went back to listening.

"Enough." Robert's voice rang through the courtyard, and Mika felt the magick in the words. "We know they are here, and we will not play your games. The families have ignored you for too many years. It is bad enough that you go around calling yourself witches and doing contaminated magick, but you have coerced the wrong family members. I have already been in communication with the other families, and unless you hand them over right now, we will join and cast a Dismembership."

"A what?" Mika said.

"What are you talking about?" Martha asked.

Vi moved away from the door, eyes wide and mouth open. Mika followed her into the ritual room.

"What is he talking about? I've never heard of a Dismembership. I doubt it's a real thing."

"It's real, all right," Vi said. "We have had one family or another threatening us with it for years."

"Then maybe it is all a bluff?"

"No." Vi hesitated. "They have cast it before, once. A Dismembership is what you cast when a coven loses their right to practice. It is usually a punishment for a coven that starts going bad or gets a lot of attention from humans. But the families don't like us much. As you have seen, we are not very traditional. It was cast in the '70s by the coven up north. The spell forces people to leave against their will. It was over five years before the magick wore off enough that they could start over. If all the families cast it … well, I imagine it will take a lot longer."

"Can't you just move and practice somewhere else?"

Mika hadn't realized that Rob had followed them.

"This is our home," Vi said. "That should be reason enough to not want them to cast it. However, it doesn't work that way. None of us will be able to work together no matter where we go."

Mika thought about Zim being pushed out of yet another home. She thought about the ease of the coven family outside and how readily they had accepted both Rob and herself.

"We aren't going to let that happen."

She turned and walked out the front door. The crowd had gathered together, blocking the doorway from the unwanted visitors, but Mika pushed through until she was standing next to Martha and her wives and joined them in facing off against Robert.

"You will not threaten this or any other coven."

"Who are you to tell me what I can and cannot do? You can't even manage to lead a ritual."

The barb no longer worked on Mika because she had led a ritual. She also now understood that she had more magick than Robert and that magick did not require the elders' rules.

"Who am I? I am the next leader of the Ember coven. Come Samhain, I am your replacement. I will lead, and you can go and give your wisdom to the elders' council. I am sure they will give it the attention it deserves."

"Where is my son?" he asked through clenched teeth.

"I'm here."

Rob looked defeated. All the vibrancy he had picked up over the last few days had left him. Mika wanted to tell him to stay behind, but she knew that it wouldn't be allowed. They would still insist that they needed to be married, and Mika hadn't had enough time to figure out a solution.

"Tom. Jake. Take them to the car."

Mika looked up and saw Tom standing over by the gate. He didn't look exceptionally pleased to have been pulled away from the elders. Next to him was a witch Mika only vaguely remembered. He was large and muscular and looked extremely nervous. Mika imagined Robert must have thought of who had the most muscle and forced him to come along. It wasn't like he could say no to the coven leader.

"That is sweet that you think we need an escort," Mika said. "But my car is only a little ways down the block. We can make it just fine."

"You are coming home with us."

"You expect me to leave my car? Can you imagine when I have to explain to the elders why I need a new one? You know how much they love spending money."

"Fine," Robert said. "Give Jake your keys. He can drive it back."

Mika walked past Robert and up to Jake, who was trying to look anywhere but at the assembled coven. With as full as the courtyard was, it didn't leave a lot of space.

"Hey, Jake." She put her hand on his arm, and he reluctantly looked at her. "Did you have to take off work for this?"

He shook his head.

"Is your boss a witch?"

"No," he said. His words were so quiet she could barely hear.

"Is he magickal?"

He shook his head. "I work at the shoe store. He's a brownie."

"Your boss is Stephon? He's a great guy. I promise to give him a call and let him know what happened so you don't get into any trouble."

"Thank you." Tears started to form in his eyes.

"Do you know how to drive?"

"Yes, I'm an O'Leary."

The O'Learys were a family that had been in Ember for

generations. They ran the main car lot in Ember, the same one Mika had gotten her car from. At the mention of his family, she realized who Jake was. Despite his size, he was only in his early twenties. Mika remembered him being a very shy kid.

"Perfect. Here are my keys, and here is my credit card. Make sure to use this for gas and food and if you run into any trouble. My car is not far away. Just go straight down this road, and it is parked on the left. It is a red hatchback with Colorado plates."

"I remember it." Jake took the items and glanced briefly behind Mika before turning and walking out the gate.

Mika looked up and saw Tom staring at her with a quizzical look. She shrugged and then turned around. "All right, Robert, it's time for us to go home."

The rental car was a gray sedan. It was a completely nondescript vehicle that would fit in anywhere. Robert and Tom paused once they reached the car, and it only took a moment for Mika to realize that Jake must have been the one to have taken the wheel. Both men seemed unsure about navigating the busy Los Angeles traffic.

Mika grabbed the keys from Robert's hand, ensuring he was aware of her annoyance, and moved to the driver's seat. Robert didn't argue as he sat in the front passenger seat but let out a series of grunts as if the situation put him out.

Rob and Tom both slipped in the back seat and instantly faced toward the window. Neither was willing to be involved in whatever fallout seemed inevitable.

Mika continued to ignore it all. She was done with posturing and proving her worth. If she was going to lead the coven, then she would do so without regret.

"Did you drive all the way here?" she asked.

"No, we flew. We will pick up tickets for you and Rob once we reach the airport."

"You were that sure of success?"

Mika pulled out her phone and found directions to the Los Angeles airport. Then, to show her annoyance at the situation, she pulled up some music and blasted it through the car. The sound of pagan folk music filled the air.

"I think it is best if we don't have that distraction while we drive," Robert said.

Mika ignored him, pulling out into traffic, letting the music wash through her.

The airport wasn't far from where the coven had been housed. But distance in Los Angeles seemed to deny the laws of space and time. Even when the car managed to move through the congested roads, they never seemed to make much progress. By the time Mika pulled into the rental car drop-off area, her nerves were frayed. She never wanted to drive in Los Angeles again. However, she made sure not to let any of that show as she reached over and handed the keys to Robert, and pressed the button to open the trunk. She stayed calm as she collected her suitcase, making sure that none of the men could see the shaking of her hands.

As the group boarded the airport shuttle, excitement settled over Mika. She had never been on an airplane before, her only knowledge having come from television. It was a bittersweet end to an adventure where she had learned more than she could ever imagine, and yet not enough at the same time.

Robert managed to pick up four tickets on a flight that left for Denver in a few hours. Her statement earlier had been meant to be a quick barb, but it seemed Robert had indeed flown them out on one-way tickets, unsure of how long it would take to bring them home. It hurt Mika's pride a bit that it had been so easy for them. Within hours of arriving, they were headed back. Mika's heart sank as she realized that they had succeeded because they had successfully threatened the people Mika and Rob had grown connected to. The only way Robert's plan would not have worked is if she had been willing to sacrifice other people. That Robert thought so little of her filled her with rage. She grabbed her ticket from the coven leader and stormed off to the security line.

Mika made sure to grab the window seat, and she spent most of the flight looking at the world from a bird's-eye view. It was saddening to see what humans had done to the planet. They pushed back nature to build squares outlined in asphalt. However, it also showed how insignificant humans were in the grand scheme of things. All it took was to move a mile up for the concerns of the world to fall away. Another mile, and they would be even more disconnected. Somewhere out there in the universe were other beings who would never even know of human existence. And yet, what happened on this planet did matter. There were billions of people all living together, and that was its own importance.

Mika's musings were interrupted by the offering of beverages and snacks. She drank down her soda and ate the pretzels with the understanding that she might never get to experience this again. Covens tended to stick to themselves, and there would be no reason for her to travel. Her place would be in Ember for the rest of her life.

When they landed in Denver, the whole experience seemed short and circular. They headed to Robert's car, where he made a point of driving. In defiance, Mika moved into the back seat next to Rob, leaving Tom to ride in the front. Robert scowled at her from the rearview mirror but didn't say anything.

It was a few hours' drive from the airport back to Ember, so they settled in. It felt right to be home. California had been a nice break, but to be back surrounded by the trees and mountains settled a part of Mika that she hadn't even known had been unsettled. Rob seemed to be having the opposite experience. The closer they got to their city, the more his shoulders slumped and his face lost the joy he had once had.

Mika reached over and tapped his arm, and then, making sure that Robert wasn't looking, she channeled a small flame in the palm of her hand. They might be back in the same place, but they were no longer the same people. Mika didn't know how, but she knew there was a way to make the coven break out from the shackles that had been holding them down.

"Do you smell fire?" Robert asked. He looked around frantically, as if expecting the entire car to be on fire.

Mika closed her palm, extinguishing the flame, and both she and Rob started laughing uncontrollably.

Mika's house hadn't changed. It was the same white walls and tan furniture. The lack of color no longer relaxed her. *Had it ever relaxed her?* Now the walls felt like they were pressing in on her. She needed to get out. It didn't matter where. Except she wasn't allowed to leave. There were witches outside watching to make sure she didn't take off again. A part of her wanted to test the situation. They were just coven members tasked with a job that they were not prepared for and which had probably not been properly explained. And who would come and get her? Robert again, at the bidding of the elders.

No, she might have come home when she had to save the California coven, but she had always meant to come back, for her coven and for Birk. Mika knew now more than ever that she needed both of them in her life.

She focused on the white of her walls and allowed the magick to fill her. It only took the smallest amount, reshaping it in her mind and whispering to it until she directed it to her living room walls. They went from white to light green. While Mika was analyzing the color, trying to decide if she should go darker, a knock on her door startled her.

She walked over to her window and pulled back the curtains. Robert stood outside.

A large part of her wanted to leave him on the doorstep. He wouldn't dare to try and enter her house, and even if he did, the wards would stop him. Not just the old ones that she had been allowed to cast. There were new ones that Vi had taught her as well. She had cast them yesterday shortly after they had arrived. There was no end of magick in Ember, and she could no longer hide it. It coursed through her, and the more they kept her locked up, the more she had found ways to use it.

Robert knocked again.

Mika looked down at her couch. She put her pointer finger on it and turned it a dark green. She compared it to the wall, and when she was satisfied that they looked good together, she walked over to the door and opened it.

"You have been summoned to the elders."

"Goodie. Let me go and grab my jacket."

She closed the door as she walked a few steps to her kitchen and picked up her jacket from the back of the chair. The air outside was warm, but Mika had long since learned not to trust Colorado weather.

She paused, looking at her kitchen table. It was light brown wood with white legs. The whole thing was boring. Mika concentrated on the wood, deepening the stain until it showed a dark brown. Then she made the legs a bright blue.

"Hum, maybe not." She adjusted the legs to be a bright yellow instead. It was different, and Mika wasn't sure if she liked it. But she turned and walked toward the door. There would be plenty of time to think about it later.

Mika didn't wait for Robert as she left the house. After she shut the door, she turned and started walking, causing him to rush to keep pace. They walked in silence for a block, nearly halfway to the coven assembly.

"Why did you do it? Why go to California and bring us back? I know you want to keep being the coven leader. You could have had it for at least another decade, or until I decided to make my own way back."

"It doesn't matter what I want. The elders have made their decision, and it is my responsibility to carry it out."

"Why?" Mika stopped and faced him.

"Why what?"

"Why do the coven leaders bow down to the requests of the elders? We are supposed to be in charge, making the hard decisions. The elders are there for counsel. When did it change that their word became law?"

When Mika realized that he wouldn't be able to give her an answer, she kept walking.

The coven chamber was empty and dark when Mika opened the door. This was another example of ridiculousness. The hall was meant to be enjoyed by all, but the light switch was on the stage near the elders' door. That had been an addition long after the hall had been first built, and it suddenly seemed very intentional. Mika threw up her hands in frustration and flicked the switch from across the room.

Robert walked in right after. He looked at the lights and then at Mika. He opened his mouth as if to say something, but before the words could come out, the elders' door opened, and Tom appeared.

"I'll let the elders know you are here. They should be ready soon."

"Wait, Tom, I have a question for you."

He paused with one hand on the door, waiting.

"Why did you come to California? I know how much it means to you to be here, making sure that they are taken care of. Why would you leave that to come pick me up states away? You had no idea when you would be back."

Rage and annoyance flickered across his face before he

calmed himself. "The elders asked it of me. I would have preferred that you had not put me in that position, but it is my responsibility to do what the elders ask of me."

"Because you are their caretaker?"

"Because I am a witch."

He stepped back and slammed the door closed.

Mika watched quietly as the elders took their places on the stage. Elder Milton fell asleep in his chair while Elder Emily kept getting up and wandering around. At the same time, Elder Sage settled into her chair like it was a throne, and Mika her supplicant. When they brought in Elder Nam, helping to adjust her frail body on the seat, it felt like Mika was seeing this situation for the first time.

Respecting her elders had been ingrained in her from a young age, and she still strongly believed in it. However, there was a difference between respecting and blindly following every word they said. They were following a rule book that had already been outdated when they'd learned the rules. Elder Sage might have been involved in the women's rights movement, but even that movement left out a lot of women. There was always room for growth, and Mika wanted to keep growing even when it was her turn to sit on the elders' council.

Having broken away for a short time made her realize how small Ember was. Yet, it was even more important that things change in small towns where everything was expected to stay the same.

"It is good of you to return to us," Elder Sage said.

"It is disrespectful that you left. This coven found you and raised you, and when things got a little too hard, you ran off. It is a disgrace," Elder Nam said.

"Disgrace," Elder Emily said.

Mika stopped listening. It all felt like a play with everyone expected to assume their assigned roles. It hit her then that their disappointment had nothing to do with her being queer. That was the target that they'd flung their anger at. Robert had probably stood through the same degradation as she was now. A part of her wondered what younger Robert had done to piss off the elders, but it didn't matter. None of this mattered because it wasn't about community but condemnation.

Robert cleared his throat, bringing her back into the moment.

"Mika has told me herself that she is remorseful and will not abandon the coven again. She is ready to face the consequences of her actions."

"I'm sorry," Mika said, following the script. "I realize that my actions have effects on the coven, and I will thoroughly think through future decisions to determine the outcomes of my choices."

Elder Nam frowned. It wasn't exactly what they wanted to hear, but even if none of this mattered, Mika was not going to lie to the elders.

"The wedding should happen at once," Elder Nam said.

"Yes," Elder Sage said. "Tom, go and grab Rob."

Tom opened the door when his name had been called and had already left the stage and started heading out into the night before Mika could reply.

"Tom, can you hold off for just a moment?" Mika said.

He looked up at the elders, uncertain what to do, but they all glared down at Mika.

"The wedding will go on," Elder Nam said.

"I understand that," Mika said. "It's just that I was

thinking about what Elder Sage had said earlier about the relationship between coven leader and spouse. Elder Sage herself was the first woman to maintain control over her magick. I was wondering how it would look to the coven if I were to take a husband before I successfully performed a ritual."

"It sounds like stalling to me," Elder Nam said.

However, Elder Sage leaned forward slightly in her chair.

"I know that I am a stronger magick user than Rob. You all know that I am a stronger magick user than Rob. I just wonder if the coven knows. What if they think the reason I succeeded was because he was leading the ritual and not because I was finally able to focus and fulfill my responsibilities?"

"She has a point," Elder Sage said. "If they think that it was Rob's doing, then they may upset the balance. They could insist on only calling male coven leaders or on having women being controlled by their husbands. It would set a bad precedent. It is much better that she completes the ritual before the marriage."

"And I should be officially called to the position before the wedding, with all the rights and privileges."

Elder Nam looked Mika over as if trying to find the angle that she was pushing. "The wedding will continue right after the ceremony."

"I understand what you would have me do. The Samhain ceremony is important to establish myself as worthy of being the coven leader. I understand now that I need a partner to successfully handle the magick that filters through the coven, and such a union will be made after the ceremony."

"Directly after," Elder Nam clarified.

"Yes, directly after."

Elder Sage stood up and conferred with the older women. Mika felt Elder Milton's gaze on her. He looked as if he could see through all of her plans. She shook off the thought. She didn't even have a plan yet, just some vague scraps that were refusing to connect. She looked back at him and gave him her sweetest smile. He let out a silent chuckle, and as the women stopped conversing, he went back to sleep.

"We still have concerns," Elder Sage said. "You have not yet regained our trust. However, we find that this direction is in the best interest of the coven, and we agree with your plan. We hope that you continue to show such wisdom moving forward."

Mika was energized by the time she made it back to her house. There was a relief in knowing that she had the space to come up with a plan. Now, she just had to figure everything out. A deep longing came over her to be back in the communal eating area, spending time with her new friends. However, what she really wanted was to break away and go to Rocko's. That was her community. Birk might even be there, and she could grab a dance for luck before she had to execute her plans. The guards had been called off after the conversation with the elders, but Mika didn't want to put anything in jeopardy by being impulsive again.

A knock sounded on her door. It was most likely Rob come to commiserate in person, but when Mika opened the door, Birk was standing on the other side. They were dressed in a pair of jeans and a red and black flannel shirt, looking every bit as good as they had on their date. Mika had to stop herself from reaching for the nymph.

"Hi," Mika said.

"Hello."

"Would you like to come in?"

Birk hesitated for an instant and then walked through the

door as if they were on their way to a battle. Then they paused and looked around.

"This isn't what I expected."

"Did you think it would be all tans and whites?"

"Well, at least clean."

After the meeting with the elders, Mika had started looking through her cupboards and drawers. There were candles somewhere; there had to be. The remnants of disorder were all over the floor. For the first time in a long time, Mika had felt free. It had been an amazing feeling.

"I was looking for something. If you give me just a minute, I can clean up."

"It's okay. I don't plan on being here long."

Something about those words dug into Mika. She didn't respond to them. Instead, she went to the couch and cleared off a pile of books so there was space for them both to sit.

Mika waved her hands, inviting Birk over, and then sat down on one edge of the couch.

"Thank you for coming," she said once Birk had sat.

"I wanted to say goodbye."

"Goodbye? Are you going somewhere?"

"Not me. You. The wedding is still on. You are still locked up in this house."

"I went to California," Mika said.

"I heard."

"I got a letter back from them, and you are right. There is so much I don't know about magick. However, I know a little more now. The elders are wrong. It doesn't rely on gender at all. It isn't about opposites, but community. You'd like it there. They all want to meet you."

"You came back?" Birk clenched their hands in their lap as if afraid of having any hope.

"I came back for you, and for the coven. I never planned to stay away. I just needed enough time to come up with a plan."

Birk scooted closer, their hands now out in front of them. "You have a plan?"

"I … not yet." Mika watched the hope fade from Birk once again. "They pulled me back before I could create one."

"The wedding is still on?"

"For now, but I'm working on a way for us to be together. That is, if you want to. I know I have done unforgivable things. I should never have pulled you in front of the elders like that without any warning. What they said to you was horrible, and it is my fault you heard that."

"I can't." Birk stood up and walked back toward the door.

"Wait." Mika ran after them. "Please don't go."

"I won't be an alternative. I know you don't love Rob that way, but if you marry him and want to sneak around with me. I just … I can't do that."

"No." Mika reached out for Birk's hand and, realizing what she had done, dropped it again. "I wouldn't ever ask that of you. Can we sit back down? I need to explain."

Mika watched Birk rubbed their hand where she had grabbed them and then rejoined her on the couch.

"I understand why you needed to leave your family. I want you to know that I not only respect that decision but I recognize it. I was right there by your side through all of it. At the same time, I was not dealing with what was happening in my own family. Going to California taught me a lot. I learned about magick, but I also learned that our coven is wrong. We are stuck in the past and I need to help push us forward."

Mika reached out, holding her hand toward Birk, waiting to let the nymph close the final distance. When their hand was inside hers, a part of her felt complete for the first time in a long time.

"I can't promise you anything at the moment, and I am sorry about that. Please know that I would do anything for my family, but you are my family as well. I am hollow without you, and I would never ask you to sacrifice part of yourself for me. You have been asked to give up too much already. I just ask that you don't lose faith in me yet. Give me a chance to find a way back to you."

"The wedding is on Samhain?"

"There won't be a wedding."

Birk looked at her in disbelief.

"Right. No promises. I will do everything in my power for there not to be a wedding."

Birk stood up, Mika's hand still in theirs. She moved forward, feeling the warmth of the nymph on her skin. Mika reached up and brushed her hand across their cheek. She wanted so much to kiss them, but it wouldn't be right, not now. So, she contented herself with the feel of them.

"Do you want to see a magick trick?"

Mika moved her hand down to Birk's shirt and felt the magick shift, changing the red to green. Birk looked down in disbelief.

"How did you do that?"

"I'm a witch, remember?"

"You did learn some things in California."

"I did. I learned that I need you."

Birk let go of Mika's hand and Mika's heart sunk. But then Birk moved their hands around her neck, standing up on tiptoe until their lips met. The kiss was as warm and sweet as she remembered. They held on to each other until there was another knock at the door.

"I'm sorry. I hadn't meant to interrupt you two," Rob said.

"You are always welcome here. Your timing was impeccable."

"I am sorry."

"No, it was good." Mika started moving around the living room, putting objects back in their place. "I need to work on fixing things on my end and we may have both forgotten that for a moment."

"They make you happy." Rob went over to the couch and sat down.

Mika looked at him. Taking him out of the California sun had sucked all the joy out of him.

"You miss it there?"

"I think I do. I like the people, but I think maybe I enjoyed people treating me like a witch instead of a conduit. When did you get a green couch?"

"This morning."

Rob raised an eyebrow.

"I changed it. I couldn't stand to be trapped in this drab room for a moment longer. How did I ever live like this?"

"You changed it? With magick? Is that possible?"

Mika looked around the living room and, satisfied that it

was in a state of order, moved to the kitchen. Rob followed behind her and pulled out one of the kitchen chairs before sitting on it backward.

"You changed the table also?"

"When I was with Vi, what were the others teaching you?"

"They taught me plenty, but mostly things I didn't know about myself, like that I am probably, most likely, aromantic. Also, I could maybe code computers and stuff like that."

"Not magick stuff?"

Mika opened up all her kitchen cupboards, digging through the contents. There were dishes in there, but since Mika avoided cooking as much as possible, a lot of the cabinet space was used for storage.

"No, why would they teach me magick? You're the one destined to be the coven leader."

Mika left the cabinets open and sat next to Rob at the table. "It isn't that simple. Did you know that they change coven leaders around, not every few decades, but sometimes years or even months apart?"

"That sounds confusing."

"I admit, it confuses me also. But they can do it because everyone can perform magick. Some have more specific skills but if you can feel magick, then you can use magick."

Mika lifted her palm, showing him her flame. "You can do this."

Rob hesitated as if she was teasing him by giving him everything he had wanted and then yanking it away at the last second.

"Trust me," she said.

He held out his palm, looking at her expectantly.

"Do you feel the flame?"

"I think so—maybe."

"Feel the energy and call it to you and recreate it on your hand. I know you can do it."

They sat in silence, the flame darting across Mika's palm.

She made it bigger and smaller, allowing Rob to feel the difference, but nothing manifested for him.

"I can't," he finally said, throwing his hands down.

"Wait, the kid said that not everyone connects to every element. Of course, fire isn't your thing. Water—I bet that's it." Mika raced to the faucet and turned on the spout, letting a stream of water out. Then she concentrated and moved the stream backward and forward until she gathered some of it into a ball, holding it in her palm.

"Did you feel that?"

"Yes ... I think I did." Rob concentrated until the water pouring down from the faucet began to waver a little. Then, small droplets separated, moving toward Rob until they fell on his hand.

Rob looked in fascination at the water, and then they were hovering above his hand again. They wobbled as he tried to find a balance until they crashed down again.

"We are taught to conserve magic, that its purpose is to be a fuel for rituals," Rob said. "Will experimenting with this power cause damage?"

Mika turned off the faucet and sat next to him. "They taught us what they wanted us to know. Maybe they believe it. Our coven is so caught up in appeasing the past that we have never stepped back and questioned anything. Magick is everywhere and available to everyone who can access it. Including you."

"Why?" His voice broke as he spoke.

"Rituals are still important. You saw what we were able to do in California. By coming together, we made real change, and not just for witches. There does need to be space to do a ritual, although not in the same way the elders have taught us. It isn't all a lie, but it does seem like there has been a lot of gatekeeping. When I am coven leader, things will change around here."

"I can't. I came here to tell you that I am leaving again. I know I can't go back to California, but I can't stay here either. I can't marry you."

"I know. I can't marry you either. There is another way out of this; I know there is. I hate to ask this of you, but can you stay until Samhain, at least?"

"You have a plan?" He looked at her with hope for the first time that night.

"Not yet, but I will. I just need to find some candles."

Rob walked over to the pantry and pulled out two quart-sized scented candles. "Will these work?"

"How did you do that?"

"I noticed them a while back when I was looking for food. Honestly, I'm surprised you couldn't see them. There isn't much else in your pantry."

Mika grabbed the candles from him, slamming them down on the kitchen counters.

"Go. Let me figure this out. Don't leave town before talking to me, and in the meantime, practice. Just not where your father can see."

When Rob let himself out of the house, Mika pushed aside the kitchen table, opening space on the floor. She sat down and placed the candles around her. It wasn't exactly how Vi had taught her, but she had said this magick was all about intention. The rest were just props to help funnel the need. Mika had enough need without extra candles. She placed one on either side of her and envisioned calling the elements. After they were invited, she lit the flames of the scented candles. A sweet cherry scent wafted in from one side, and a spicy autumnal scent from the other. It was not a pleasant combination, but Mika did not let that deter her. She sat focused on the flames and her need.

There had to be some way through this. She needed to set Rob free and allow the possibility of her and Birk. In addition, there needed to be a way to bring the coven forward, letting them all be free to experience magick. Mika felt the energy flow through her. Since she had stopped blocking the force, she had felt freer and happier than she could ever remember. It was like she could take a full breath for the first time. She wanted that same experience for her coven.

Mika sat still, meditating on the problem until the candles started to disappear. All at once, her eyes opened, and the flames blew out, leaving a small trail of smoke. Mika had a plan.

Mika looked at the wedding dress in the mirror. It fit perfectly, and if she had the chance to choose, she would have picked something similar. She wished she could keep this dress and wear it if she ever did get married, but she knew that she couldn't. There was too much emotion attached to this dress, and none of it was beneficial for a marriage. With one last final look, she walked to the seamstress and allowed her to unhook the dress. She pulled her blue cotton skirt and light blue shirt back on and looked at herself in the mirror again. She appeared plain, almost boring. But that was better than a union that was not meant to be.

When Mika walked out of the large fitting area, she saw Rob being measured for his tux. He was flushed, shoulders slumped, staring at the ground.

"Hey," Mika said.

Rob turned, nearly knocking over the tailor helping him. "Are you supposed to see me before the wedding?"

Mika rolled her eyes and then turned to the witch with the measuring tape. "Do you mind giving us a minute?"

The man looked up at Mika with a starstruck expression and moved to the back room without saying a word.

"We should probably talk quietly. I have a feeling that he is back there eavesdropping."

"What does it matter? It is not like there is anything to hear."

Mika poked her finger at his chest. "Do you have so little faith in me? I told you I would figure out a plan, and I have. Do you still want to go to California?"

"I can't go back. I couldn't put them in danger."

"You can go back if it wouldn't put them in danger."

Rob straightened up, as if unwilling to believe but also unable to stop the hope. "I can go?"

"I'm working things out, but I will be able to get you to California without anyone even knowing. Pack a bag. Don't let your father catch you, but also don't plan on coming back unless you decide to. I should be able to ship your things, but I can't promise. I'm not sure how your father will take it."

"Take what?"

Mika just smiled at him. "Pack a bag and pretend you are still getting married. I'll give you more details later, but if everything goes right, you will be out of here before Samhain."

As Mika left the shop, Rob almost looked like he believed her.

Mika wasn't even the coven leader yet and was already exhausted. There were a million things to organize.

She had been allowed out of the house without supervision as long as she didn't leave the town. It was nice to have a little space, even if it was just as she walked from the bakery back to the coven house. The menu was at least taken care of. There would be plenty of sweets to celebrate. Not that the children needed any more. There was a mountain of bags of candy already back at the coven house.

The day was warm. Mika hadn't even bothered with her

jacket and there were plenty of people walking down the main area of town. She waved hi to those she knew but kept walking, unwilling to lose her freedom again before the start of the ceremony. When Dave's sedan turned onto the road, Mika moved down an alley between two large buildings on instinct. Some part of her knew it would be Birk behind the wheel learning how to drive.

They handled the car like a natural, even if the speed limit was 25. They pulled into a spot near Rocko's and the duo got out of the car and headed inside. Mika hadn't talked to Birk since they had visited the house a few days before, and she wanted nothing more than to walk inside and ask to join them for lunch. But she couldn't, at least not yet. Mika just hoped that when everything was done, Birk could forgive them for everything she had put them through. But that would have to wait. If Mika went to Birk now it would ruin everything. No, she had to continue to play the dutiful witch.

With a slight tear in her heart, she turned away and continued walking toward the coven house. The witches went all-in on Samhain, and the yard was full of hay bales and games. There were at least a dozen witches outside decorating. Inside was no less spectacular, even if it was more formal. The tapestries had been brought out of storage and hung on each wall. There was one for each element, appropriately placed on their corresponding wall. The stage was lined with jack-o'-lanterns brought in by the families. Orange and black fabric draped across the ceiling, transforming the drab plaster into elegance. Various black metal stands stood around the room. Most were tall, looking more like vines with shelves sprouting off them. On each of these offshoots, there were candles. They had all been replaced with electric ones after an incident a few years back where one of the candles had been bumped and a witch had sustained some burns. However, on the night of the ritual they would still flicker, providing the expected ambiance.

The elders sat on the stage, presiding over all of the decorating, even though it was Robert and Mika's responsibility to make sure everything was taken care of. Robert's wife was placing the last of the candles on stands while Robert was finishing setting up the altar for the ritual. Mika headed over to help him and update him on her tasks.

"You made it back," Elder Sage said.

Mika repressed a groan and walked over to the stage.

"Of course she came back," Elder Nam said. "She now understands her responsibilities to the coven."

"We do have a way of bringing wayward witches back into the fold. I remember when I was preparing to take the mantle of coven leader and the elders tried to make me a figurehead. I fought with everything I had until I understood the wisdom that they brought to the coven, and took my place."

"I am glad you have returned home," Elder Nam said. "Now remember that we have the best interest of the coven in our hearts. We make these decisions from love, and in time you will come to understand why."

Mika stood frozen, trying not to let the shock show on her face. In every story, Elder Sage had stood up and demanded her right to lead the coven and now she was advocating meekness. Mika made eye contact with Tom as he was supervising Elder Emily. For a brief moment, she realized he understood the absurdity of the moment. Then he turned away. Mika returned her attention to the elders.

"Thank you for your wisdom. I should go and help Robert now to make sure everything is ready for the ritual." She left without being dismissed.

Robert had finished laying out the offerings and placing the candles—real ones this time. There was not much else to be done, but she followed him around just to avoid having to go back to the elders.

"What did they make you give up?" Mika asked.

Robert started, as if unaware that she was even there.

"When you became coven leader, what did they make you give up?"

"I have not given up anything. Being coven leader was all that I had ever wanted."

Mika picked up one of the candles, holding it gently in her hands. "There was nothing that you would have done differently if you had been given a choice?"

Robert glanced briefly at his wife on the other side of the room.

"Was there someone else?"

"When I was younger, I had a fling with someone."

"Who?"

Robert stopped moving and turned to talk directly to Mika.

"You wouldn't know her. She moved shortly after my marriage. Her name was Mary and she had the most beautiful blue eyes I have ever seen, but she didn't have much magic. The elders decided my wife and I were a better match. We have dutifully served the coven for several decades."

Mika put the candle back on the altar, making sure it was securely in its holder. "They tried to make Elder Sage give up her independence. As much as she is all for us listening to the elders now, I don't think she did when it was her turn."

Robert walked up to Mika, getting very close. "Don't. Do not ruin this ritual. The coven deserves a leader who will respect and guide it."

"Perfect. That is exactly what I plan on doing."

Mika strode across the room to one of the children who was helping to decorate. It was the youngest Thompson kid. They were always eager to help and impeccably dressed, from their shoes to their perfectly plaited hair.

"Would you like some help?"

He nodded.

Mika lifted him, allowing him to place the candle.

"Want to see a magick trick?"

He nodded again.

Mika felt the energy around the candle, causing it to light up. It was easier than she thought to manipulate the electricity, so she reached out and turned on every candle in the room.

"Wow," he said.

Mika put him down and looked around the lit-up room and saw Tom studying her again.

There were more than a hundred adult witches packed into the coven hall. They were decked out in their most elegant clothing. Women were mostly in dresses, and men in dress shirts or the occasional suit. Most were standing, as there was only limited seating for those who needed it. The elders had plenty of space on the stage, but no one would even think of asking to join them, so those gathered stood shoulder to shoulder, happy to participate in magick, even if it was just as a filter.

Only adults were allowed inside. The children were still at home with babysitters or outside being minded by the teenagers. They would be anxiously waiting for the ritual to end so the celebration could begin. The sound of their play was blocked out by the thick wooden walls.

The area around Mika was also clear. There was only the altar full of the tools that she would need. Rob stood behind her, dressed in a long flowy gray robe similar to what his father wore, only his had a hood that covered his head. He stood still, eyes focused on the ground, fulfilling his role as conduit.

Robert and his wife stood in the crowd close to the altar,

ready to jump in if Mika failed again. She knew she wouldn't fail.

Mika was dressed similar to Rob, except her robe was a silky red and her hood was pulled down, letting everyone see who she was and what she was about to do.

She stepped up to the altar and let the magick fill her. It coursed through her body like electricity, making her alert and aware. She picked up the athame, a long slender silver knife, and pointed it toward the north.

"I call upon earth, which gives us dependability and a firm foundation. Please join us."

The green candle on the north section of the altar ignited.

She moved the athame to the east.

"I call upon air, which gives us intelligence and inspiration. Please join us."

The yellow candle on the east section of the altar ignited.

She turned behind her and pointed toward the south.

"I call upon fire, which gives us passion and determination. Please join us."

The red candle on the south section of the altar ignited.

Then she turned toward the west and pointed the athame at the blue tapestry.

"I call upon water, which gives us intuition and healing. Please join us."

The blue candle on the west section of the altar ignited.

The power of the elements rushed through her. She took a moment to allow them to flow through her freely and then set the athame on the altar before raising her hands in the air.

"Samhain is a night where the veil is thin, and we can connect to all those who have gone on before us. We ask them to hear us, and invite them to join us. We have brought gifts for you to enjoy."

Mika looked down at the altar that was decorated with a sampling of food that had been brought for the feast later that night. This food would stay untouched for the next day to allow the ancestors to enjoy it at their leisure.

"Ancestors, we ask you for your wisdom. You have seen so much change in your lives and your deaths, and we ask that you help guide us to a future that will bring the coven not only prosperity, but also wisdom, and charity toward others."

Mika paused, allowing the feeling of magick to flow through everyone in the room. The words were not completely to the script that had been spoken for as long as Mika could remember, but no one would question it. At least not now, in the middle of the ritual. After, there would be too much else for them to be concerned with.

The magick began to build within her until it pulsed through her body. Then she went completely off script.

"We are witches. We have a divine connection to the basic structure of the universe. We can call upon it in partnership and love because we are bonded. Ancestors, we ask you to help us find the legacy that we have lost and to build our community stronger than it was before."

In the center of the altar stood an empty black cauldron within which, at Mika's words, a fire raged, its flames reaching a foot above the edge.

The crowd let out a collective gasp and then, as if ashamed of their reaction, became even more still.

"Tonight I will take on the role of coven leader, handed down freely from Robert to myself."

The ceremony was supposed to take place after the ritual in a private ceremony, followed by an announcement to the collective, and Mika had prepared for that plan. However, with the magick flowing through her, it no longer felt right to exclude the coven from a rite that impacted them.

However unexpected the situation, Robert stepped forward to fulfill his role.

"I, Robert Sandleman, relinquish my responsibilities as

coven leader and hand them on to Mika—may she serve the coven well."

"I, Mika Lowe, accept this responsibility and promise to serve this coven to the best of my ability. I will take on the mantle of leadership and devote my days to the service of our community. I promise to respect the traditions of our people while working toward the acceptance of all people. I will devote myself to learning about our connection with the universe and bringing this knowledge to everyone with the gift."

Mika raised her hands again and this time, for dramatics, a piece of the flame rose into the air. Next, a small sphere of water rose from a cup on the table, followed by a stone. She moved them around until they were spinning in a vortex, each item just a streak of color before the coven's eyes. She looked out at the people and saw them all watching in fascination and some concern. Mika dared a glance toward the elders and saw the looks of dissatisfaction on their faces. But there behind them was Tom, decked out in a suit, eyes wide and twinkling as he watched, mesmerized.

Slowly, the wind stopped, and the elements once again separated. Mika lowered them gently back to the table and picked up the knife, thanking and dismissing the elements one by one until the ritual had ended. Before the room filled with chatter, Mika spoke one last time.

"Let the celebration begin."

The doors were flung open, and parents went out to join their children. Some of the adults stayed talking in hushed voices, eyes darting between her and the elders. But as Mika slipped toward the open doors, she caught a few enthusiastic whispers.

"That was so cool."

"How do you think she did that?"

"Do you think I could do that?"

Mika was outside watching the festivities when Tom found her. He stood next to her as they watched the children, dressed in costume, running around from game to game to win candy. Even now, the air was charged with magick. It gathered around the group as if asking to be noticed.

"That was some ritual," Tom said. "It seems you learned a few things in California."

"Did you know?" Mika looked up at Tom as she asked. "All that time you spend around the elders, did they tell you they were hiding the truth about magick?"

Tom took a deep breath but didn't answer. Mika turned back as they watched their community celebrating. In the distance, there was a large bonfire encircled by teenagers who had been given their own supply of food to have a party within the larger party. Mika remembered those awkward years when she was trying to understand why it was never one of the guys that she wanted to tug into the trees to kiss.

"The elders say a lot of things. They have talked about how things used to be and how things ought not to be, but it is not always easy to understand what they mean, especially when they do not want you to understand. What you did …

when you turned on the lights ... and created the flame ... can anyone do that?"

Mika opened her palm and created a flame. It caught the crowd's attention. Some turned away, choosing to pretend that it hadn't happened. Others moved closer, pretending not to hear. As Mika talked, a few stopped pretending altogether.

"Not everyone can conjure magick. At least not every human. Magick is part of the fabric of the universe and being able to sense it and utilize it is what makes us witches. Some people have a stronger connection and will naturally be able to utilize magick more efficiently. However, every witch can do something. Most will be more connected to a specific element. They may not be able to conjure a flame but they can manipulate earth, water, or air. This is part of our heritage."

"A heritage that they hid from us."

"I don't understand their motivations. Maybe it was fear, greed, or perhaps the understanding of who we are kept diminishing with the generations. All I know is that I intend to start holding classes tomorrow for anyone interested." Mika turned and faced the growing crowd. "Just know that, like everything in life, there are consequences and responsibilities that will come with learning. The Treaty of Ember prohibits exposing the magickal community to humans, and that will be an even greater temptation the more you learn. There is also a risk that comes with the elements. Magickal fire is still fire and will act as such if not controlled. I have faith in all of you, so if you are interested, meet me at my house tomorrow evening."

The group started to break up then, and even those who were pretending not to listen moved into smaller groups, talking amongst themselves while they watched the children. Mika was going to create a special group just for the children. They would be the first modern generation to grow up with actual magick.

"The elders sent me to find you," Tom said

Mika let out a laugh and patted Tom on his arm. "I would hate to disappoint them."

Only a few dozen adults remained in the coven hall. There was a group that was working on bringing the food from the back kitchen, and there were the elders still sitting on their thrones. A few adults, including Robert and his wife, had gathered around to talk to them. Even growing up, Mika never understood why the elders stayed away from most of the coven. She had been the only child to visit their rooms. Even when their family visited, they moved out to the coven hall. They very rarely left the building once they were called to the council. At least Robert would be keeping his house for the next few decades and would be able to help connect them to the community.

When Mika made it to the stage, Tom shouted for everyone to leave. The adults looked briefly startled but did not question the command. They quickly finished what they were doing and left the room, closing the doors behind them.

"You called for the celebration," Elder Nam said.

"There was supposed to be a wedding," Elder Sage said.

"Wedding," Elder Emily said.

Elder Milton sat wide awake, watching but not speaking. His eyes stayed focused on Mika, more alert than she had ever seen, as if there was finally something worth staying awake for.

"Where is Rob?" Elder Nam asked.

"He's not here," Mika said.

"Where is your son?"

Robert looked around the room like he would magically appear. "I can go look for him."

"You won't find him," Mika said. "Rob left this morning. He has removed his claim of membership in the coven and is free to find another family or to remain without a coven."

"Balderdash," Elder Sage said. "He was here just an hour ago. We all saw him in the ceremony."

Mika walked to the door and opened it. The hooded figure entered, noticeably shorter than during the ceremony.

"I would like to introduce you to Vi."

Vi removed the hood, revealing her short blonde hair and a wide grin.

"Nice to meet you all," she said.

"Vi is joining us from the California coven. She will be my second."

"No!" Elder Nam tried to rise, but her frail muscles caused her body to shake. Tom was next to her in a heartbeat, trying to help settle her back in her seat, but she kept shaking in frustration. "I will not allow that abomination in the coven. You will not get married to another woman."

"I am not marrying Vi."

The elder stopped fighting her caregiver and turned her attention back to Mika.

"Vi and I are magickal partners. When you taught me that leading a ritual required a partner, you were correct. However, your insistence that my partner be another gender and that we must be married was incorrect. Vi will be a very important part of my life and in this coven, but we will not be romantic partners."

"What have you done?" Elder Sage said.

"I think I did much what you must have done when you became coven leader. You were not going to stand by and be used like a puppet during your administration and I will not either. Just like it was wrong of the elders to deny females rights in coven leadership, it is wrong that you deny those of us who do not conform to your expectations. I am gay. I am proud to be gay, and I will no longer hide that part of who I am."

"But you will not marry her?" Elder Nam asked.

"No, I will not marry Vi. What I will do is date Birk, if they are willing. And maybe we will marry if it is right for both of us."

Elder Nam tried to get up again, but Tom was already at her side to stop her from hurting herself. The screams that came out of her mouth were incoherent and slightly muffled by his large frame.

"I think it is best that you go and rest," Tom said.

"I will not leave while the coven is going to shambles."

"As caregiver, it is my responsibility to keep you safe. If you keep up this exertion, then you will cause yourself harm. It is my duty to stop that from happening."

Elder Nam looked at him in disbelief. The realization that she could no longer have her every command blindly followed slowly sunk in. Mika felt bad for the older woman. She knew that one day, she would be in the same situation with an aging body, requiring the aid of others. Mika would have to repair the damage she was doing to the elders, but she wouldn't stop. Who knew how many others in the coven were being damaged due to outdated thinking?

"I will keep myself under control."

Tom nodded and stepped back just behind her chair.

"In my brief time in California, I learned more about magick than all the years of your tutorage," Mika said. "The most important thing I learned is that I did not have to keep my guard constantly up against magick's power. It is a part of me, as much as any other aspect, and by closing it off, I was losing a part of myself. You taught me that magick was a finite resource that could only be pulled out during rituals. I understand the importance of rituals and the good that large magickal workings can do. However, it is just as important that we maintain our connection to even the smallest aspect of the craft."

Mika lifted her hand. Lighting a flame had become nearly effortless, and she was excited to start training with Vi to understand her capabilities. However, this small demonstration was enough to elicit gasps from the elders.

"I am aware that you know this is possible. I do not know if you have the training yourself, and I don't think it ultimately matters. What does matter is that, starting immediately, we are going to teach our witches how to use magick."

"You cannot," Elder Nam said.

"Why?"

The elders exchanged looks, communicating wordlessly in a way that only came with strong intimate bonds. But finally Elder Sage voiced their thoughts aloud.

"That is not how it is done. Magick should not be used frivolously."

"That is not a good enough reason."

"You do not get to make these decisions," Elder Nam said.

"She is the coven leader. I handed over the claims, and now she leads us. It is her right to make these decisions, just as it is your right to counsel her about them." Everyone turned and looked at Robert, surprised that he had spoken up. "My place is now on the council, so I must also provide my wisdom. What she did tonight—I didn't know any of that was possible, and I have been leading our people for decades. What have we been missing out on? What have you kept to yourselves, unwilling to share with those around you?"

"You would have been told," Elder Nam said.

Mika paused to process what she had heard. They had known and kept it among the elders. It was time to change that. "Starting tomorrow, we will be teaching those who wish how to do magick. You are all welcome to join. It will be at my house around dinner."

Robert frowned at Mika skeptically. "I will be there. We will also make sure there is food."

When Mika laughed, Elder Nam's and Elder Sage's faces both soured.

"You have made it so I cannot go to my rest in peace,"

Elder Nam said. "How long must I stay around to make sure the coven is in good hands?"

"Elder, I believe I speak for us all when I say we will be happy to have you around for as long as you can stay," Mika said. "I hope that you find peace before your passing."

"I want to go," Elder Milton said.

"Go?" Elder Sage said.

"I would like to attend the training tomorrow. Tom, would that be possible?"

"I would be happy to take you," Tom said.

"I would like to go to bed now," Elder Nam said.

Mika waited as Tom helped the elders to their chambers. It was impossible to miss the animosity that radiated from Elder Nam and Elder Sage. Mika chose to focus on the new joy she saw in Elder Milton. Elder Emily walked beside him as they left the stage.

"Fire, fire, fire," she sang.

"Thank you," Mika said when they had left.

"I followed the rules," Robert said. "I gave my life to their expectations. They were all lies."

"You did what you thought was right for the coven. No one has ever doubted your intentions. Now you will continue to do so."

"My son?"

"You will leave him alone?"

Robert nodded solemnly.

"He went back to California to join their coven. He has friends there who are not tainted by his role of being my shadow. He wants to go to school to learn how to program computers."

Robert looked back at his wife, who had stood silently throughout the entire conversation. Even now, she focused off into the distance as they talked, not joining in.

"Maybe that's for the best," he finally said. He took his wife's hand in his own as they walked toward the exit.

Mika turned toward Vi. "Welcome."

"That went better than I expected."

Mika grabbed the other woman in a hug, not stopping the relieved laugh that flowed through her.

"Did Zim settle into the house?"

"The kid took the bed. I'm sleeping on the floor until we can find our place. She decided to try and do the awkward introductions by herself. I checked in on her after the ritual, and she was hanging around the bonfire talking up some girl."

"I'm glad. If there are any problems, let me know. It'll help smooth both your transitions as much as possible. For now, I have one small favor."

"Go," Vi said. "I'll monitor the rest of the celebration and the cleanup. Go see about your person."

A grin spread across Mika's face, and she didn't wait another second as she launched herself toward the door.

ocko's was full of adults decked out in costumes. There were humans in witch costumes and werewolves in cheap werewolf costumes. A few clowns strolled around, and many of the women were in clothing that was a lot shorter than they typically wore in public. In the middle of it all was Birk, sitting at a small table working on their computer.

They were dressed in a dark blue suit with a purple shirt and a blue tie. Mika wasn't sure what they were supposed to be … maybe a business person? But they looked amazing. Mika hesitated, her confidence waning. She had no right to beg Birk for their forgiveness, but the thought of losing them without at least trying was too much. They pushed through. Most of the people were already so drunk that they were barely standing, and moved out of her way easily enough.

Then Birk was right before them, so focused on their computer that they didn't notice.

"Excuse me, is this seat taken?"

"I need it. I'm meeting someone." They didn't even bother looking up.

"Oh," Mika said. She stood there, uncertain what to do next. "I'll just leave you alone." She started making her way back through the crowd when she felt a hand encircle her wrist.

"I'm sorry. I didn't know it was you," Birk said.

"I can leave you alone if you are busy."

"Please sit."

Mika pulled out the chair and sat awkwardly. She couldn't remember the last time she had felt this out of place in Rocko's. Birk finished typing and then suddenly closed their computer.

"I'm sorry, I had to finish a little bit of work."

"No need to apologize. You didn't know I would be here." Mika rubbed her hands on her thighs, trying to overcome the awkwardness. This was not the reunion she had pictured, but to expect Birk to fall right into her arms was not realistic either. "Work is going well?"

"It is. I actually have a meeting soon."

"Oh."

"I wanted to keep busy tonight. I didn't want to think about everything. Did you become the coven leader?"

"I am. The ritual went well."

Birk leaned forward. "You're married?"

"No."

"You're getting married?"

"Maybe, eventually. But not to Rob. He moved to California."

Birk looked so cute with the confused expression on their face, and Mika wanted nothing more than to reach out and grab their hand, but she held off.

"Rob wanted to move to California, where he could start over and find himself. I met a witch in California, and she moved into the coven to be my second."

"Oh," Birk said. "That is great. I'm sure you will be happy together and I'm glad you found a way for them to accept who you are. I need to get back to my work so I'm ready for my meeting."

Now it was Mika's turn to sit there confused, uncertain what she had done to make Birk so upset.

"We aren't together, Vi and me," Mika said.

"You said that you needed to be in a relationship to handle magick."

"That is what the elders told me. It turns out that they lied about a lot of things. Vi is very queer, but I'm not interested in her like that, and she knows my heart belongs to someone else. A very special person who gave me the strength to question and to seek out new answers."

"Yeah?"

"Yes. Now, I just need to ask if they could ever forgive me for the ordeal I put them through. I am sorry."

"What exactly does this mean?" Birk asked.

"Birk, would you like to go out on a date with me? No hiding this time, with the coven's full knowledge."

"They gave you their approval to be with me."

Mika ran her hand through her hair. "Not exactly. I don't think they will approve, but I did make them aware that if you agreed, then this is how things would be. Every second that I was away from you, I felt like I was missing a part of myself. All I could think about was fixing everything so that we could be together. I know what we have is still new, but if you will have me, then I am all in."

Birk stood and held their hand out to Mika. Mika placed her hand inside and stood up, pulling Birk closer to her. When their lips met, magick poured through every cell of her body, and the way that Birk clenched her shirt made Mika think that some part of them felt it as well.

Cheers erupted all over the bar, but Mika tuned them out. She had been away from Birk too long to give anything else her attention.

Except … there was a wolf standing too close, watching them. It was not anyone Mika had seen before. She reluctantly pulled back.

"Is there something I can help you with?"

"I'm Len ... I mean Lennon. I have a meeting scheduled with Birk." He stood awkwardly, one hand in his khakis and the other clenched tightly to a small suitcase. His eyes darted around the room as if he was expecting an attack at any moment.

Birk turned around and extended their hand. "Len, it is nice to finally meet you in person. This is ... well ... this is Mika, the local witches' coven leader. She also is my girlfriend."

Mika's cheeks flushed at hearing those words. She wanted to wrap Birk in her arms and take them back to her house. Except Birk had a job to do.

"Mika, this is Len. He is a representative from the organization that is funding the conservation work I am doing."

Mika held out her hand, but the man completely ignored it.

"There are wolves here? There is a coven and a wolf pack here?"

"There are many people in Ember, including humans," Mika warned.

"Right," Len said. "I didn't realize this meeting would be so public. Maybe there is somewhere a little safer we could go?"

His eyes kept darting back toward the group of wolves. Most of them were ignoring him completely, too busy getting drunk and playing darts against the pixies. One wolf, however, was staring at him directly. Mika recognized Ancel immediately. He was Phoenix's friend and usually the gentlest of the wolves, but his gaze sharpened as if he had just found prey. Suddenly, Mika could not fault Lennon for his fear.

"Don't worry," Birk said. "Rocko's is neutral territory. Even the vampires know better than to cause a scene in here.

This is the safest place you could be in Ember. If anyone gets out of hand, Rocko will handle it."

"Then maybe I should just never leave," the man muttered.

"I should go," Mika said. "Will I see you later?"

"Tomorrow?" Birk asked.

"Tomorrow."

Mika leaned down and gave Birk a quick kiss and then headed toward the door. She turned back to look again at her … partner. The word was still so new and so uncertain. Tomorrow, she and Birk would decide on the correct terminology.

The new wolf's gaze kept darting back and forth between Birk and Ancel. He was visibly shaking. Until Ancel suddenly stood up and rushed to the door, pushing past Mika on his way out. Lennon seemed to breathe for the first time in minutes, but his eyes were still a little too wide, and his hands shook slightly.

That one has a story, Mika thought as she went into the night. There was still plenty of time to head back to the celebration and be there to help clean up.

Get a FREE Short Story!

Join My Newsletter

Sign up at mj-james.com

www.ingramcontent.com/pod-product-compliance
Lightning Source LLC
Chambersburg PA
CBHW070514200726
48293CB00007B/2527